THE GOD GAME

BY

D. RON MACK

Dedication

There are some people I would like to thank for their help in making this all come to fruition.

To Dan Cantin, one of my oldest and dearest friends, I want you to know how much I appreciate your support and friendship. Your encouragement in the early days of my writing was something I needed, and you gave it freely. Bless you!

To my friends, guides, mentors, and all around wonderful people, Dr.s Andy and Heather Yates, I love you! You have been my inspiration, as well as that little voice in my ear constantly reminding me to get it done. You have changed my life. Your compassion in dealing with a wounded soul has been a marvel to behold. I want to be you when I grow up.

Prologue

It had been a long trip and Jhama was tired. He had been cursing himself and his belief in these stupid dreams for the last 300 miles. Damn the Sisters and their teachings! It was they who had drummed into his head the need to believe in dreams as a child in school. He often found himself trying to deny his belief in The Book of Life, but with little success. The Sisters of the old God "With No Name" had done their jobs well in his case.

He had grown up in a small village in the northern reaches, where the village elders had been virtually ruled by the Sisters of Loruh. It had been a childhood filled with many memories of good people and good times, memories that he cherished greatly now in the 50th year of his life. Much as he might hate to admit it, the teachings of the sisters had a lot to do with this. Their dedication to the spreading of the Word and the teachings of peace and brotherhood had profoundly changed the history of his people.

No one knew exactly where and when the Sisterhood had begun. It had always been rumored that they had come from somewhere high in the mountains of the island nation of Sul. Of course, when anyone queried one of the Sisters on this matter, they would always smile and say that when we deserved to know, Loruh would lead us. If anyone persisted in their questioning they only got the inevitable lecture on the virtues of patience and attention to our dreams, always this emphasis on dreams. Is it any wonder then that, after half a lifetime of this teaching, he would finally start having strange dreams?

It had started about six months ago. Of course, he had dreamed all his life, just as all people did. These were not the dreams that the Sisters talked so much about. Their teachings spoke of dreams of such clarity that one would truly believe they were in a waking state. They talked of learning to enter these dreams on command, of being able to fly, and to control one's dreams. This was what had been happening to him. It had been very unnerving in the beginning. Yet, he had been taught all his life that this was possible, so he had come to accept and even enjoy it.

Then, one night everything had changed. There had been a voice that had spoken to him from thin air; a voice that shocked him, so that he awoke from his dream, only to find that the voice had followed him into the waking world. This voice had called him by name, and chilled him to the bone.

"Jhama! Your life it about to change beyond your wildest imaginings. You are poised on the verge of one of the single greatest events in the history of your world, but you are not ready yet. You must complete a long and hazardous journey to a Holy place. There you will receive knowledge that even the Sisters do not posses."

He jumped from his bed and quickly searched his house. He could find no one, which, of course, did nothing to reassure him. He returned to his bedroom and quickly knelt down on the floor next to his bed. Closing his eyes he prayed to Loruh to protect him.

"Get up, Jhama. It is not your worship I crave, but your obedience."

Slowly he opened his eyes and stood up. He was becoming more frightened by the moment. Silently he prayed, "Loruh, is that truly you?"

Immediately the voice answered, "Who else could know your thoughts?"

Trembling visibly now, he spoke aloud.

"Why me, Great One? Who am I that you should so honor me?"

The voice began laughing and said, "Ancient is that question. Once it was spoken by a man named Moses, who lived so long ago and so far away that it is beyond your comprehension. All your questions will be answered, but the time for such things has not yet come. So, therefore, set your affairs in order and prepare for your journey. Long is the trip you must undertake and you must leave by tomorrow morning. Hurry! The God we both serve awaits you."

"But where do I go, Great One? What place do I seek?"

"Lie back upon your bed and you shall know."

Still filled with fear and apprehension, Jhama returned to his bed. As he closed his eyes, he fell immediately into a deep sleep. Slowly before his mind's eye unrolled a map of what appeared to be his world. Jhama had seen maps before, but never one so beautiful and detailed. He saw his village as a small dot of light blinking off and on. From this point, a line of golden light spread slowly across the map. Southwards it ran, winding its way out of the highlands and into the great desert; from there it ran eastward to the coast.

Still it continued due east across the reddish waters of the Sea of Hemat, until it reached the Island of Sul. Straight into the mountains it went, with ever smaller details becoming visible on the map. Slowly, the entire route was revealed to him, until he saw an old, stone temple rise before him. There the map disappeared and he drifted off into regular sleep. The last thing he remembered from this dream was the words, "Make Haste!" drifting across the map as it faded out.

When he awoke from the dream, he no longer questioned it. So, his journey had begun the next day. Four months had past, one of them at sea. He had been wending his way through the Holy Mountains now for three days. The map of his dream had been burned into his memory and he had never faltered. Every detail of his trip came to pass exactly as he had seen it. He knew he was near the end now. Just over the next rise should be the temple he sought.

As he reached the front of the temple it began to glow softly with a golden light. The entire building was made of what appeared to be one solid block of stone. Not one seam could he find nor any sign of an entrance. Slowly he circled the building twice, but could find no trace of any way to gain entrance. Finally, he sat down on the ground and started laughing. All these months he had traveled and all the dangers he had faced, just to reach a building he had seen in a dream, which would not let him in. As his laughter ran its course, he wiped the tears from his eyes and stood up.

"Well, Great One, that was quite a joke on me. I suppose this was intended to teach me some kind of lesson, but I'll be damned if I know what it is. So what now? Do I simply turn around and go home again?"

Suddenly he heard a loud cracking sound like the splitting of stone. He turned to stare in disbelief as a large vertical crack appeared in the front of the temple. He watched as the crack grew into the outline of a large set of doors. Slowly then the doors swung open as he heard a new, male voice saying, "The lesson here is patience, Jhama. Come, you have much to learn."

Inside the temple Jhama saw a large wooden table filled with food and drink. Next to this was a smaller table with one chair and a large book in the center of the table. Back toward the northern end of the building was what appeared to be a bed. Placed at intervals along the ceiling were large, glowing orbs that provided a soft, gentle illumination for the entire structure. The rest of the building appeared to be empty. The strangest thing of all was the fact that even though the temple appeared to be ancient, not one particle of dust could be found. It was if the building had been sealed off from the rest of the world from the time of its making until he had arrived. Once again the male voice spoke.

"Sit, my child. Eat and refresh yourself. The food will be replaced as often as needed and the bed is for your use. The book you see before you is the reason you have come. Read it! When you are done, we shall talk again."

Slowly Jhama approached the book. He sensed that he would never again be as he once was, if he opened it. Yet, this was why he had come. This was what the dreams had led him to. He really had no choice now, and he knew it. He sighed and thought back over all that happened to him. Where did it all start? He laughed to himself as he reached for the book. Of course he knew where it all had started. It began with the dreams. That phrase echoed through his mind as he opened the book. His blood froze in his veins as he read the first sentence.

1.

In the beginning, God dreamed the world into existence. Over it's surface did his spirit fly.
The Book of Life

It began with the dreams. Like most people I dreamed nightly, but I seldom remembered them. Lately, however, that had all changed. At first they were about the normal types of things you would expect, such as work, my kids, sex. The only thing unusual about them was that I was remembering them and they were becoming increasingly vivid. I also began to have more control over what happened in the dreams. The hunted became the hunter and the victim the victor. Then, I began to fly.

It was difficult at first because, like all kids from my generation, I had watched Superman fly on television. You know the routine. Take three running steps, then jump! This wasn't the same at all. You kind of make yourself lighter, and lighter, and spread out on the wind. It was more like being a kite than actual controlled flight. I went where the wind took me. The fear of suddenly regaining my weight or losing the wind and falling kept me very close to the ground, in the beginning, but that did not last for long.

I soon found that I could control the direction and speed of my flight, by manipulating the "wind." I also found that instead of flying face down in a horizontal position with my arms stretched out in front of me (sorry, Superman again), I could fly standing up, upside down, on my back, on my side, or any combination of the above. Gravity ceased to have any meaning for me. In fact, none of the normal laws of physics seemed to apply. Making a turn could be done in a graceful, sweeping arc like a plane, or I could simply change direction ninety degrees, instantaneously, at a thousand miles an hour, with no ill effect or strain. I could now hover at fifteen thousand feet in a blizzard and remain totally comfortable. The wind did not ruffle my hair. In fact, the "wind" that sustained me in my earlier flights seemed to gradually disappear altogether. Most unusual of all, the dreams were becoming as real to me as my waking life.

I found myself thinking about these dreams constantly during the day. I could hardly wait to go to sleep each night to get back to this new reality, where I could be so free. I found that I could get to sleep as early as eight o'clock with no problem. This had been almost impossible most of my life. I was a night owl. I preferred to sleep during the day and stay awake all night. There was something surreal about the way the world looked at night, and I was more imaginative and creative at 3:00 AM than I ever was at noon. That certainly seemed to be true now. Nothing I had ever conceived of during the day had ever been as imaginative as my dreams had become.

I was now visiting all the places I had always wanted to see, but could never afford to go in my waking life. The volcanoes of Hawaii had always fascinated me. I had seen many nature specials on PBS about them. However, nothing I had ever seen on TV ever prepared me for the sight of an active volcano at night, hovering fifty feet above the cone. The noxious fumes that would have overcome me very quickly in reality seemed to simply pass right through me. I felt no heat at all from the liquid rock bubbling and squirting so close below me. The color of the magma was beyond description; sort of a cross between orange and pure gold lit from within, with a dark, grayish black crust around the edges.

I was concentrating so hard on the sight inside the volcano that it took me totally by surprise, when a sudden gush of magma was thrown practically in my face. My instinctive reaction was to cringe and close my eyes. I was shocked and very relieved, when the lava simply passed through me and shot about a hundred feet over my head. As I looked up and saw it complete its arc and start to fall, I shifted my position slightly and reached out my hand. I was thinking how much fun it would be to be able to catch the lava in my hands and mold it. Imagine my surprise as a large globule of the magma fell into my hands, and stayed there, with no heat, no burning, and no pain.

Becoming bolder with this success, I suddenly wanted more. I stretched out my arm towards the lava below and an even larger piece of glowing, steaming, liquid rock came towards me. I added this to the first sample and formed it into a sphere about two feet in diameter. I found that I could make it fly, too. I played with it for some time, making it hover, dip, and float. As I tired of this game, I finally sent it up about five hundred feet and exploded it like 4th of July fireworks. Intense? Not nearly as intense as my shock, when I saw the news the next morning.

It seems there had been some strange things happening in Hawaii last night. I sat and kept repeating "Oh my God!" over and over again, as I watched the footage shot by a volcanologist at the same time I was dreaming the night before. What the hell is happening? There on the screen before me unfolded the drama I had played out in my dream. I was sure I had finally lost what little grip I had ever had on reality, as I watched the fireball float slowly around the sky, apparently all alone. Then it finally shot straight up and burst into streamers above the volcano. The reporter assured us that the experts all agreed that what we had just witnessed was impossible according to all the laws of science. Ufologists claimed it was the best UFO footage to date. The Millennia freaks claimed it was another sign that the end was near. Many Hawaiians claimed it was simply the goddess Pele strutting her stuff. Me? I was just plain scared.

How could this be? It was just a damn dream, wasn't it? Dreams can't affect the real world. So, what was the explanation then? I decided it must be one of those psychic things that happen to us all every once in a while. I had some kind of vision, saw what was going on in Hawaii, and my brain filled in some details to make the dream more entertaining. I'm not sure why the thought that I could be having prophetic dreams was less scary than the possibility that my dreams could somehow manifest themselves in the real world, but it worked. I blew it off and went about the normal drudgery that is my "real" life.

That night I went to bed somewhat later than I had for quite a while. I was a little nervous after the experience of the previous night. Who wouldn't be? Still, once I fell asleep I felt that same giddy euphoria as my feet left the ground. I went up to about ten thousand feet and flew lazily above the desert for a while. It was so peaceful being suspended there with the stars above and the lights of Phoenix far below me. I started thinking about what had happened the night before. There was a way to prove that it had only been a coincidence. I could try to leave another visible trace on the real world and see what happened when I woke up, but let's do this on a less spectacular and more private scale this time, just in case.

I flew back down to the city and over to the Papago Buttes. There was a small cave there, not really much more than an impression in the rock, that I was familiar with. I found a small stone there and carved the words "No way" on the back of the rock wall. Laughing, I flew off and played in a thunderstorm over Flagstaff for the rest of the night. I had a ball playing Zeus and casting thunderbolts. I did some target practice on an old dead cactus at the top of one of the mountains there.

The next day, I drove over to the Papago Buttes after work. I parked my car and looked up to locate the spot, where the little cave was. I was chiding myself all the way up the hill, for even expending the effort it took to climb up there in the hot sun, to check on a dream. As I reached the top, I paused and lit a cigarette. I took a few puffs and caught my breath, as I looked out over the valley. The sun was just going down and producing one of those sunsets that look like something out of Arizona Highways magazine. Why was I stalling? I did not want to have to go back down in the dark. It was not a terribly steep descent, but there were a lot of areas with loose rock and a bad fall out here by myself would be inconvenient at best.

I turned and walked to the cave and looked toward the rock wall, where I had scrawled the message in my dream. Even in the desert air, I suddenly felt a chill go down my spine. There it was, just as I had seen it in my dream, with one exception. Just below where I had written "No way," in a totally different handwriting, were the words "Wanna bet?".

I stopped at the liquor store on the way home and picked up some good old Southern Comfort, 100 proof. I didn't even bother with any Coke to mix it with. I just took it home and drank it straight from the bottle. Since, the best way for me not to think about something, I can't deal with at the moment, is to turn on the TV and veg out, that's just what I did.

The evening news was on and I was about half way through the bottle, and just starting to feel numb, when the weather report came on. The meteorologist was saying something about the possibility of more rain in Flagstaff tonight. He then proceeded to tell the story of the violent thunderstorm that had taken place the night before. It seems that one spot at the top of a mountain there had been hit over thirty times by lightning. No one had ever heard of such a thing. He said it seemed almost as if the lightning had been aimed at the same spot over and over again. I finished the rest of the bottle rather quickly, and went night-night even quicker.

I awoke the next morning with all the blessings that one would expect to be bestowed by a whole pint of 100 proof, consumed in half an hour. I fixed myself a breakfast of aspirin and coffee, and slumped down on the couch, to wait for the kettle drum concert in my head to end. In the midst of my misery, it suddenly hit me that I had not dreamed last night. At least, I could not remember doing so. It must have been the booze. It either stopped me from dreaming, or it kept me from remembering. Anyhow, my head hurt too much right then to try to figure it out.

I stayed home from work that day and allowed my body to slowly eliminate the poisons, which I had pumped into it the previous evening. By the time the sun was beginning to set, I was almost back to normal. I ate a light supper and, to my great relief, it stayed down. I finished it off with a cup of hot cocoa and lay down on the sofa with a sigh of relief. With the headache gone, my belly full, and the hot cocoa caressing my chocolate zone, I closed my eyes.

I was back in one of my favorite spots again, hovering over Phoenix at about 10,000 feet. I was horizontal with my eyes toward the stars. I seemed to draw strength from the glow of the city lights below me and the slow dance of the stars eased my mind.

"Beautiful, isn't it?"

I let out a yell and shot straight up about 100 feet, whipped around, and looked back towards where the voice had come from. There, floating slowly towards me, was a woman, giggling and waving at me. She looked to be in her early twenties and was clothed in a simple white dress. It was very short, revealing two perfect legs below, and small, well-shaped cleavage at the top. Her hair was a light, golden color and about collar length. She was about 5'7" and had the largest light blue eyes, I had ever seen. She had full lips and sculptured cheek bones, a tiny, pert little nose, and a chin that was almost pointed. The overall effect was overwhelming and instantaneous. She was the most beautiful woman I had ever seen.

This must have been very apparent in the way that I looked at her. Still smiling, she stopped about three feet from me and said, "Uh-oh. I smell testosterone in the air."

"My dreams are getting better," I said. "I don't know why I haven't thought of this before. This will be much more fun than playing with lava," I said as I reached for her. Instead of closing my fingers around the soft skin of her wrist, as I had expected, my hand bounced off a very hard and very invisible wall around her.

"Not so fast, big boy. I may be your dream girl, but I'm as real as you are. There will be time enough for that after we get to know each other better and you learn a little control. You've been more than a little flashy lately, haven't you?"

"Who are you?" I asked. "You are the first thing I have encountered in any of my dreams so far that has not obeyed my every whim. What's the deal?"

"My name is Laura. I'm your ... well, advisor will do for

now. My first piece of advice is, get over this dream nonsense. This is no dream! Haven't you figured that out yet? I would have thought your message in the cave and my addition to it would have settled that. I am trying to help you understand what is happening to you, before you start drawing some unwanted attention to yourself. Make no mistake; there are some people out there who would gladly stop at nothing, to find out how we do what we do."

I sighed and looked at the two of us hovering quietly in mid air and said, "Okay, if this is not a dream, and I guess I'm beginning to believe that it is more than that, then what is going on? I sure as hell can't fly when I'm awake!"

"Are you sure?" she said. "When was the last time you tried?"

I laughed at first, but she was giving me an odd, measuring sort of look. I swear, I got the impression that she was trying to decide if I was mentally deficient or just had a warped sense of humor.

"Are you saying that you think I can?"

"I'm not sure yet" she said with that same serious expression. "However, I don't recommend that you try it for a while yet. It could be monumentally dangerous, for a lot of reasons I'd rather not go into right now.'

'Your whole world is about to be turned upside down. You will find that almost everything you ever thought you knew about life, and mankind's place in the grand scheme of things, is wrong. How long it will take you to get beyond the initial shock and get on to learning how to control your powers, and how to protect yourself, will depend entirely on how well you listen. You must have faith that, at least for now, I know what is best for you."

I floated there silently for a while, staring at her. There was an odd mixture of youth and naiveté, with strength and surety of purpose in this woman. My past associations with women had not been very satisfying, starting with my mother. Her religious fervor and downright fanaticism had led her to denounce her own son before her church, as demon possessed. If the truth be known, it was mainly because I refused to let her run every aspect of my life, like she did all the members of her church.

My choices of girlfriends and finally a wife had not fared any better. I seemed to gravitate towards strong women, who seemed to feel as if I were somehow inadequate, because I was so easy going. They also insisted on running my life for me, but seemed disappointed in me when I let them. In the end, it was always the same. I love you, but I just want to be on my own for a while. Like I had somehow held them down or controlled them. By the time I reached my late forties, I had more than had my fill of the faithlessness of women, but that did not stop me from appreciating their beauty and occasionally lusting after one. I would really have to watch myself with this one!

"So, we will be spending some time together," I said. "Being close to such a beautiful woman could be very pleasant. I do, however, reserve the right to tell you to take a hike, if I don't start getting some answers that make sense and can be proven. I also want to warn you that if this is going to involve sitting around chanting, you can forget it. I do not have the patience to spend 10 years learning to contemplate my navel. Nor am I interested in anyone's religious views. I will join no cult that worships anything or anyone other than me."

For the first time I saw a look of genuine warmth and good humor come across her face. It was almost as if I had just passed the first test. Maybe she had finally decided that at least I was not mentally deficient.

"You're learning!" she said.

2.

<u>And the One became</u>
<u>the Three. And</u>
<u>they were the</u>
<u>Ancient, the</u>
<u>Ethereal,and the</u>
<u>Discovered.</u>
<u>The Book of Life</u>

We talked for a while longer and agreed to meet outside the dream state. She said she already knew where I lived and she would meet me at my place at 6:00 PM. She then just kind of faded from sight and was gone. I suddenly thought about how my "dreams" normally ended. I did not remember making a conscious effort to wake up. It was more like one minute I was flying and the next I was waking up in my bed. I decided to go back home and do something that had never occurred to me before.

I found my complex with no trouble and floated up to the door of my apartment. I hesitated there for a moment trying to figure out how to get in. I knew the door was locked, since that is the last thing I check each night before going to bed. I shrugged and just moved through the door as if it were a mist instead of solid oak. I glided through the living room and down the hall toward the bedroom. I reached the end of the bed and stood there for several minutes looking down at the sleeping body.

It gave me the weirdest feeling that I had experienced to date. There was the same face I saw every morning in the mirror, while I was shaving, but this was totally different. I knew it was me, but somehow this guy looked older than I thought he should. As I walked around the edge of the bed to get a better look, I was suddenly shocked to see a complete stranger on the other side of the bed.

It was a young man in his early twenties with light brown hair down to his shoulders. He was about 5'10" tall, with a 42" chest and a 30" waist, lean and well muscled. He was the kind of man I always envied, because he looked the way I would have liked to and never could. I had just enough time to wonder quickly who he was and what he was doing sneaking around my bedroom, when it hit me. What I was seeing was a reflection in the full length mirror on my wall. I looked quickly around to locate the guy and found that there was no one in the room except me and me; that is, awake me and sleeping me. I looked back toward the mirror and found his reflection staring straight at me. This was a little unnerving since no one but Laura had been able to see me in my dream state before.

I reached up to scratch my head and so did he. My mouth dropped open and so did his. I pointed at him and he pointed back. I was beginning to feel as if I were trapped in some bad burlesque routine, when the truth finally dawned on me. I felt like the chimp in a research project, when he finally realizes that it is not another chimp behind the glass, but his own image he is seeing. As if I wasn't confused enough already, being in the room with me and me, there was now me three to contend with.

I walked over to the mirror for a closer look. As the initial shock wore off, I began to see that the basic facial features were somewhat recognizable. There was a family resemblance there that could have made the face staring back at me a younger brother or even my own son, but no way was this a face that had ever looked back at me from a mirror before.

I looked down for the first time at my hands and arms. As I flexed my hands, I saw muscles stand out and ripple that looked like steel bands. My chest looked as if I had been pumping iron ten hours a day for the last twenty years. How could I not have noticed this before? I guess we are all so used to the way we look that we rarely actually look at ourselves. That probably explains why, when we see ourselves on a video tape, we are so surprised at how we really look. Understand, I was not upset that my appearance was so much improved, but how many such shocks can one person take in a day? Enough! No more today! I floated up horizontally over the bed, and came slowly down on top of, and finally into my sleeping body.

I woke up back in the body I was used to seeing. I know this because I checked, the minute I got out of bed. I finally seemed to be alone with only one me again. I got ready for work slowly, and then sat down with a cup of coffee and a cigarette. In the light of day much of what had transpired last night seemed easier to absorb. I was still confused, but it did not seem so overwhelming. The last thing I wanted at this point was to have to go to work and try to concentrate on insurance claims, but dreaming had not yet paid any of my bills. I still needed some way to pay the rent and buy groceries.

As so often happened, when I started thinking about work, I began to daydream about what it would be like to win the lottery. To finally be able to do what I wanted in life without being a slave to the 40 hour work week. The last time I had checked, the lottery was at thirty two million. Maybe it was time to buy another ticket. It's too bad that my dreams couldn't give me the winning numbers, or could they? With all the other strange things I had been doing lately, why couldn't I travel forward in time just a few hours and get the lucky numbers?

The more I thought about this the more involved my daydream was becoming. It should be easy to do. I had learned to bend and shape space and matter to my will in the dream state; why not time? I wouldn't even have to leave the house. I could just shift time slightly out of phase, slip through the rift this created to 9:00 PM, turn on the television, and watch the drawing. All I had to do then was memorize the numbers, slip back to "normal" time, buy the ticket, and boom, instant multi-millionaire!

I became so excited at this prospect that I stood up before I remembered the coffee cup sitting on my knee. I waited to hear the sound of it hitting the floor, but it never came. I turned to look for it and saw me number one sitting in the chair, coffee cup still perched on his knee. Me number two laughed, took the lit cigarette from the fingers of me number one, put it in the ash tray, and set the coffee cup back on the table. I looked in the mirror, waved at me number three, and reached out with my mind. I began to see these thin, glowing lines that I seemed to recognize as the time lines, sorted through the strands for the one that felt right, twisted it slightly, and stepped into 9:00 PM.

I turned on the TV to channel 12 and watched them draw the numbers for the lottery. The smiling host said the jackpot had gone up to 52.3 million dollars. I watched as one by one the little ping pong balls rolled down the chute and the numbers were revealed, 2, 7, 23, 25, 32, and the power ball was 17. I repeated the numbers to myself several times so that I wouldn't forget them. I then reversed the previous process and found myself back where I had started out. There was me number one still staring blankly into space, while me number three and I grinned at each other like we had just swallowed the canary. I backed into me number one, merged with him, got up from the chair, and wrote down the lottery numbers before I forgot them. This was going to be one trip to the convenience store that I would not mind making.

I stopped on the way to work and purchased one ticket with the magic numbers on it. I am not sure why I went to work that day, except that I thought it might help the day go by faster. The people around me had no idea why I was humming all day. Things that normally would drive me up the wall had no effect, except to tickle my funny bone. I made the comment to one of the Managers that they never really appreciated what I did for the company on a daily basis. I remember saying that someday I might just walk out and they would find out how valuable I was, the hard way.

She sneered at me, as if she knew that I could not afford to go elsewhere. This really did crack me up, so much so that I could not stop laughing. She did not seem to appreciate my sense of humor very much. She shouted, "Get back to work" at me and stalked off, as I made obeisance to her, still laughing uncontrollably.

The rest of the work day went by with much the same kind of inane crap that normally marked the passage of one more day in my life. I resisted the temptation to quit that day. I wanted to make sure that I really was about to become independently wealthy, before I gave up my only means of support. In my younger days, I might not have been so cautious, but I have paid the price for my recklessness more than once.

I rushed home to tidy up around the apartment, before Laura arrived. Of course, she might not show up at all. I was still very confused about the whole thing. Considering the circumstances under which we met, that was understandable. She was absolutely the most stunning woman, I had ever seen. That in itself was reason enough not to trust her in my book. A woman's reliability seemed to be inversely proportional to her beauty; at least, that is the way it had always worked in my life. Unfortunately, that never seemed to stop me from taking the chance of getting hurt every time a pretty woman paid any attention to me at all. I was determined that this time would be different. After all, I seemed to finally have some power. There couldn't be too many of us, who were able to do the things I seemed to be doing lately. She had sought me out or I would never have known she existed. That had to mean something.

There was a knock at the door. I nervously checked the mirror to see the condition of the remainder of my hair, glanced quickly around the apartment one last time, and opened the door. There was a woman, I had never seen before, standing there. I looked at her for a moment and said, "Yes? Can I help you?"

She smiled at me and said, "Yes, you can let me in out of the heat."

I smiled back and said, "Now why would I want to do that?"

"Because I'm so beautiful?"

I looked at her again, smiled, and thought to myself, "Oh brother! This is just what I need with Laura on her way, a nut with delusions of grandeur."

She wasn't exactly ugly, but beautiful was hardly the descriptor I would have used. I said, "Look lady, I don't have time for this. I am expecting someone any minute now, so have a nice life," and started to close the door. She smiled and said, "Do you always act this way on a first date? I'm Laura," and held out her hand.

I must have looked like a pole-axed ox, standing there with my mouth hanging open. She laughed again, took my hand, and said, "You didn't exactly look the same the last time I saw you either. May I come in?" I stammered something like, "Yeah, yeah, sure, come in," and continued to stare at her.

She was about 5'6" with brown hair and blue eyes. She was wearing a purple skirt and white blouse, which had a rounded neck line, and was trimmed in a lacy material. Her shoes matched her skirt and were suede. She also wore glasses that seemed to enlarge her eyes. While she was nowhere near the male magnet that I had seen last night, the overall effect was certainly not repulsive. She was cute and well dressed. So, I closed my mouth, grinned at her, and finally said, "Please, sit down." She accepted my offer of some cinnamon stick tea and I started talking to her, as I rattled around the kitchen preparing it.

"I guess I should have realized you might look different than the last time I saw you. I had quite a shock, when I came home still in the dream state, and caught sight of my reflection in my bedroom mirror. This is all still quite new to me. I am not sure what the rules are, or if there are any rules at all. I hope you can shed some light on this whole thing. I could really use some answers that make sense for a change."

I brought the tea into the living room, set it down on the table in front of us, and sat down next to her. She reached out and took my hand and held it between hers. She seemed to be one of those people that liked to touch. Good, I liked that kind of person. God knows, there is far too little physical contact between members of our society today. She smiled and said, "You poor baby. You have every right in the world to be confused. It hasn't been too long ago that I was going through the same things, you are now. That is one of the main reasons I am here, to give you some answers. Where would you like to start?"

"How about at the beginning? How am I suddenly able to control my dreams and affect the material world from the dream state? Earlier today, while I was fully awake, I seemed to leave my body and made a short jump into the future and back again. Accepting for the moment that I have not gone completely off the deep end, what is going on? Where did these powers come from?"

"You've time traveled already? My God, you're right! You need answers now. There are a lot of names for what you are doing. Astral Projection is the most common, but none of them fully describe the truth. You are indeed leaving your body behind and traveling in what we will call, for lack of a better term, spirit form. So far you have found that you can be invisible to a non-spiritual presence, levitate at will, move through solid objects, move and shape physical objects, and travel through time. This is just the tip of the iceberg.'

'There are many other things you are capable of that you have not discovered yet. Although, at the rate you are going, it would not be much longer before you made the ultimate discovery on your own. That one piece of knowledge can be dangerous to your mental health, if there is no one around to put it into perspective and fill in the rest of the puzzle for you. The truth is, there is literally nothing beyond your capabilities now, in this plane of existence. This is no joke, I assure you. You have powers that most people would say makes you a god.'

'Please note that I said, in this plane of existence. There are many others, where you would be nothing more than a helpless infant. It is very important that you not come into contact with any of these planes, until you have learned much, much more about who and what you are. There are rules that must be followed, just as in the world you have been used to. The main difference is that in some of these other dimensions, there is no second chance. Intrude where you do not belong, break a rule, or just blunder into the wrong place at the wrong time and you could be destroyed utterly. Worse yet, you could also cause the destruction of others like us and those we protect."

This was way too much to swallow. Me, a god? This girl must be totally loony tunes! I started laughing. Quietly at first, then louder, with tears running down my eyes. I looked at Laura and that look was back again. She appeared as if she were leaning back toward her mentally deficient opinion of me again. Instead of causing me to become more serious, her look of stern disapproval only sent me into new spasms of laughter. When I finally was able to get myself back under some control again, I wiped the tears from my eyes and said, "I'm sorry, but this is just too much. I was just trying to picture a bald, overweight god that couldn't afford a car payment."

Her expression changed abruptly and she started laughing too. "Okay, okay, stop it. I agree that this sounds like I just escaped from a mental institution. I don't blame you for needing proof. I guess some demonstrations are in order. Come with me!"

She closed her eyes and leaned back on the couch. I knew what she was doing, so I did the same. I willed myself out of my body, opened my eyes and looked around for her. She was standing over by the door waiting for me, looking exactly the same as she had when I first met her. She smiled and said, "We can travel anywhere in the universe and in any time we wish. Where and when would you like to go? Pick a place and time you know intimately, so you will be sure I am not just providing a show for you."

I thought about this for a few moments. I gave her a date and time, and the place was an apartment in San Diego. She asked no questions. She just took my hand, closed her eyes, nodded her head, and we were there. She looked at me and said, "What happened here?" I smiled sadly and said, "You'll see. Let's go in."

Still holding hands, we drifted through the door and up to ceiling height, to get a full view of what was going on. There below us was a much younger version of me getting ready for work. My ex-wife was there in the bedroom watching me, as I finished tying my tie. She followed me through the apartment, as I went in to kiss my two young children good-bye, just as I did every morning. Smiling, she walked me to the front door, kissed me good-bye and said, "I love you honey, I'll see you tonight," and I walked out the door, got into the car and drove off.

Laura looked at me and said, "Shall we follow you in the car?"

"No," I said. "There is nothing worth watching happening to me this day, until I get home again. What I wanted to see was what happened here after I left."

As soon as my car was out of sight, my ex-wife became a flurry of activity. She picked up the phone and called someone and told them that I was gone, and to start bringing over the boxes. She then pulled the kids out of bed and started getting them dressed. There was a knock at the door, and in came the manager of the apartment complex with a bunch of empty boxes. She continued to haul them up to the apartment, while my ex-wife filled them with everything she could fit into them.

Laura looked at me and said, "Is she doing what I think she is doing?"

"Yes," I said. "There won't be much of anything left by the time I get home tonight."

"Did you know this was coming?"

"No, it hit me like a ton of bricks, when I got home. I had no clue."

"Why did you want to relive this?"

"You said I had god-like powers. I want to be able to look into her mind, while this is going on, to be able to hear and finally understand what she was thinking. I have wondered and guessed at her motives for years. I thought that maybe if I could understand, I could forgive her for what she did to us all."

"You can do more than just listen in on her thoughts. You can actually enter her body and feel what she is feeling. You can live the entire experience, as if it had happened to you. Just be careful to experience only and not to influence her thinking in any way. She could become aware of your presence and you would not get the true sequence of events, as they actually happened. In fact, it might drive her mad. You can change the past, but now is not the time for that. The consequences are far reaching and you are not ready to deal with them just yet. I'll stay with you until you are ready to go back home, and then we can talk."

I nodded and closed my eyes. I reached out with my mind toward the woman that I had shared my life with for so many years. I felt her presence and merged with it. What a mess her mind and emotions were. Her adrenaline was pumping so much, it was a wonder she did not explode. Fear was uppermost in her mind. She was deathly afraid that I would return home unexpectedly and find out what she was doing. She was afraid that she would not be finished in time for her flight. She was afraid that I would find out where she was going and come after the kids. She was afraid that I would find out about the old boy friend she had been having an affair with, and that she was running back to now.

She was not physically afraid of me, although that was the official excuse she was using with everyone. She was afraid of the truth. She was afraid of having to take responsibility for her actions. She was afraid of what the kids would think of her years from now, if they ever discovered the truth about why she had deprived them of the father who loved them, and that they loved. She was afraid that her old boy friend might change his mind and not want her anymore. Most of all, she was afraid I would catch her in this and she would have to look into my eyes. She was afraid she would have to actually see what she had done to me. She was scared to death that I might talk her into staying.

"Please God, don't let him come home until we're gone." she prayed. "I couldn't stand the look on his face. It would kill me! I don't want to hurt him, but I have gone too far to back out now. How can I love him and do this to him? I'm so confused. I just have to get away and try to think this through. Please help me! Please help him. God, help us all!"

I couldn't stand any more. I severed the contact between us and found Laura there waiting for me, as she had promised. She asked me if I had gotten what I came for. I shook my head no and said, "All these years! I have hated her all these years and dreamed of revenge. She broke up a 15 year marriage, stole my kids from me, and I wanted to hurt her. Now, when I finally have the means at hand to get all the revenge I could ever desire, I can't do it. She has hurt herself more than I ever could. I actually feel sorry for her."

With tears streaming from my eyes, I turned my back on the woman I had loved for so many years and quietly gave up my hate for her. I reached for Laura and said, "Let's go home."

Silently she came into my arms and took us back to my place. I opened my eyes and looked straight into hers. She looked at me for a long second and then kissed me like I had not been kissed in a very long time. She sighed and said, "I have searched for a man like you all my life. People who know how to love are more rare than diamonds, and worth much more. There is a thing we can do, to learn about each other. If you agree, you will know everything about me, and I about you. Nothing can be hidden. I am willing to do this with you. Do you wish it?"

I thought about my resolve not to get involved with this woman, when I first met her. It didn't last long, did it? I looked deep into her eyes and the last of my resistance disappeared. I took a deep breath and said, "Yes, I wish it!"

"You will not be sorry." she said. Gently she placed her lips against mine and the world dissolved.

We seemed to merge for a time and shared the sum total of our lives. Every memory, every longing, every dream was there and open to us both. We shared it all, the good and the bad. I felt words welling up inside me that seemed to come from a ritual I had always known, and had just now remembered. Together we spoke the words that we knew would bind us together for all time.

"Now that I have found you, I will no longer settle for anything less. You are me and I am you. Never again will we be alone. Never again will we want for love or understanding. Never will I leave you! For now and forever, I love you."

We kissed again and then opened our eyes and smiled at each other. I asked, "Did we just get married or something?'

"Yes, my darling, or something. We are now bonded to each other more deeply than any marriage could ever produce. I know you are not sorry about it anymore than I am."

I grinned so much, my face was starting to hurt. "I've never felt better about anything I have ever done in my whole life. Every fiber of my being is celebrating the fact that I have finally found the type of love I was beginning to believe could not exist. We need to move in together right away. I do not want to be away from you ever again."

"Okay, do I move in here or do you move in with me?"

"Tonight, we stay in the Honeymoon Suite at the Hilton. Tomorrow, we buy a new house together."

She giggled and said, "My, my, Mr. Moneybags! When did you become rich?"

I looked at my watch, smiled, reached out and pulled her to me, and said, "In about fifteen minutes," and kissed her.

3.

<u>Deeds of the spirit</u>
<u>will bring you riches</u>
<u>beyond measure.</u>
<u>*The Book of Life*</u>

Together, we watched the drawing of the winning lottery numbers. I produced the ticket with the same numbers on it and did a little dance in the middle of the floor. We were rich! Not just well off, or comfortable, but really rich. I had just won $52,300,000.00 that would be divided up into payments of $2,615,000.00 per year, for the next 20 years. Laura asked if that was what my time trip was about. I said that it was, and asked her if I was violating some kind of unwritten law, by using my new abilities for my own personal gain. She laughed and said no; that was not one of the rules. It turned out that she had done much the same thing about a year ago. Between the two of us, we were now obscenely wealthy.

We decided to go out for dinner and talked as we drove about plans to get married in the conventional sense. We agreed that we did not want a big wedding, even though we could afford it. We decided instead to fly to Las Vegas and get married there. Over dinner, we decided to live in Arizona in the winter and in Colorado in the summer. Laura already had a very nice home about 30 miles northeast of Phoenix. I would buy the home in Colorado, when we found the right one. I was thinking of somewhere in the Colorado Springs area. I loved the idea of being able to live close enough to the city, to be able to do our shopping without an hour's drive each way, but still far out enough to ensure some privacy.

We arrived at the Hilton Hotel about 8:00 PM and checked in to the Honeymoon Suite. The man at the front desk seemed a little taken aback that we had no baggage, but when Laura produced a Gold Card, everything was fine. When we got to our room, we lay down on the bed together and she said, "Okay, we're alone now. Go ahead and ask your questions. I'm sure you have plenty."

I thought about it for a second and asked, "You said there were others like us. How many are there, and what makes us different from the average person?"

"There are close to one thousand of us altogether on this plane. As to how we are different, technically, we are not. We are humans, just like everyone else. Everyone has the potential to be like us. The difference is in spiritual maturity. Reincarnation is real, but it does not work quite like most people believe. We are born and reborn from one life to the next, until we reach a point where these powers begin to manifest themselves.'

'It never takes the same amount of time for any two people. For some, one life may be enough. For others, it may take hundreds. There is nothing anyone can do to help a person shorten the time this process takes. It is an individual growth rate that cannot be altered. You can tell a person that they have these abilities, even demonstrate your powers for them, but it only scares and frustrates them. It is always best to leave them alone until they start to manifest their abilities."

"What happens next?" I asked. "Are we free to do whatever we want, or are there responsibilities that come with these powers?"

"It is up to you, to a large extent, what you do with the rest of your life. We are free to simply enjoy ourselves, live out the rest of our lives in leisure, or take on new challenges. Once our life ends on this plane, we must begin our new responsibilities. For now, there is no rush."

I moved closer to her, started unbuttoning her blouse, and said, "That's good to hear. Because, for what I have in mind right now, I surely do not want to be rushed." She actually blushed, but she wriggled closer and said, "I'm glad! If we get too tired to continue later on, we'll just pop out of our bodies and make love in spirit form. I've always wanted to try that, and now we can find out what it's like, together."

We passed the night in a closeness I had never experienced before. We became lovers, friends, and lifelong companions. I don't believe either one of us will ever forget that night, no matter how many millennia we might live. There was no competition, no holding back, no selfishness, and no misunderstandings. Each gave and received in equal measure. We spent a lot of time just holding each other and talking. There was a feeling of completion and wholeness, as I held her. For the first time, I knew I was no longer alone, and never would be again.

We chartered a flight to Las Vegas and were there in just about an hour. We checked into a hotel and went out looking for a wedding chapel. We managed to find one that was a little less "Vegas" than the rest, and made our reservation for that evening. We got the license, went shopping for some new clothes and rings, had something to eat, and were back at the chapel by 7:00 PM. The service was short and simple. By 7:20, we were legally husband and wife.

As the minister completed the ceremony, I felt as though we were being watched. I turned to look behind us and saw what appeared to be a whole room full of people watching us, and smiling. The funny thing was, they were almost completely transparent. When the minister said, "I now pronounce you husband and wife." I had the feeling that they were all cheering. No actual sound was heard, but the effect was unmistakable.

I looked at Laura and arched my eyebrow in their direction. The minister said, "You may now kiss the bride." and Laura whispered, "Later!",and kissed me. As we walked out of the chapel, it was kind of unnerving to have transparent rice thrown at us by nearly invisible people, which not only passed right through us, but through the floor as well. Laura laughed and said, "They are friends like us that you will meet later. They just wanted to share our joy and wish us well."

I said, "I assume they will not be showing up in our hotel room, unannounced. I have been known to be a little kinky on occasion, but I don't think I'm ready to have others watch, while we make love just yet."

I heard laughter and suddenly saw a man standing just a few feet away from us. He walked up and hugged Laura, and still laughing, grabbed my hand and shook it. He said, "Never fear, my new brother. We will give you all the privacy you want. I'm Laura's brother, Dan. I'm very happy for you both, and glad to finally meet you. Laura has been watching you for some time now. We knew you were about to become one of us and she has talked of nothing else for months. Now that she has finally trapped you, welcome to the family!"

"Watching me for months?" I said. I looked at Laura and she was blushing again.

"Thanks a bunch, Danny," she said. "Now he'll have an ego the size of Texas for the next hundred years." She playfully punched him on the arm, and then hugged him again. "Seriously, Danny, I'm so glad you could be here. Thank the others for us, and tell them we will all get together soon."

He kissed her on the cheek and turned to me. "I know you two have things to do and places to go, and I have some business to take care of, so I will leave you alone for now. We can get together later on and have dinner. I look forward to getting to know you better. Until then, take care of my baby sister, and congratulations!"

"Thanks," I said, "and don't worry, I won't let her out of my sight!"

I asked Laura how Dan had known that we were getting married and where. She said that this was another one of our abilities. We can communicate over long distances, telepathically. While we were flying to Vegas, she had slipped out of body long enough to contact Dan and tell him we were getting married. She did the same thing, while I was trying on clothes earlier in the day, to tell him where the ceremony would be held.

He, in turn, had contacted the others I had seen at the wedding. They were close friends of the both of them, and had attended in spirit form, because they did not have time to get there the conventional way. Dan, who lived near Lake Tahoe, had gotten there just in time to catch us coming out of the chapel. He had watched the ceremony in spirit form during the taxi ride from the airport.

We wandered around town for a while, taking in the sights. We tried gambling for a while, but the fact that we did not need the money, which we might win, somehow took all the excitement out of it. We finally went back to the hotel and up to our room.

I asked Laura if she would like me to order some champagne. She said no, and asked me if I remembered what happened the last time I had been drinking. I said yes, I passed out and slept all night. She asked if I remembered whether or not I had left my body that night. I did remember noting the next morning that I had not dreamed. She said that alcohol in large quantities and certain drugs could keep us from being able to leave our bodies. For that reason, most of those like us stayed away from booze and drugs.

"So what's the big deal if you get drunk once in a while and sleep, instead of leaving your body at night?"

"As I told you before, there are some people who would go to great lengths to find out how we do the things we can do. If you are drunk or stoned and pass out, you cannot leave your body and cannot protect yourself from these people. As long as we can separate from our bodies, we can protect ourselves from anything an earthbound person can try to do to us. However, if you are using any drug that keeps a person from dreaming, you are trapped in your body until the drug wears off. That can be dangerous."

"Who are these people and how do they know about us? I thought you said that what we do cannot be taught. If that is true, then why would anyone try to capture us? If we can't teach them, then what purpose would it serve?"

"As to whom they are, there are several different agencies. They work for the governments of several different countries, including our own. They are ruthless people with no conscience or scruples. They do not believe that these abilities cannot be taught. They also believe that everyone is like them. It is inconceivable to them that someone could have such abilities and not be consumed by ambition. They think of us as threats to the security of both their country, and their way of life. If they cannot control us, then they feel we absolutely must be destroyed."

"How could they possibly know about us? They can't see us when we are in spirit form. I still have trouble believing what has happened to me. Why would they?"

"About 30 years ago, one of us decided that he could do a lot of good for a lot of people, if he worked with our government. He believed that together, they could end the Vietnam War, peacefully. He had been in the Army and had spent a year there. What he had seen during that time affected him deeply. He could not understand how so-called civilized people could slaughter each other for no real reason. It weighed heavily on his conscience that he had been a part of it, even though he had little choice at the time.'

'He went through the change about six months after he came back to the states. He told some of the others what he wanted to do. They warned him that this could be very dangerous to him and a lot of others as well. They tried to convince him that there were other ways he could help, without revealing himself and his powers, but he was sure he was right and that everyone else was just overly cautious.'

'One day he flew to Washington D.C. and got himself a hotel room close to the White House. He left his body and went straight to the Oval Office, where the President was having a meeting with the head of the CIA at the time. He materialized right in front of them. He explained who he was and what he wanted to do. He levitated objects around the room, and popped in and out of visibility, until they were convinced that he was indeed what he said he was. He told them where he was staying and the President said that he would send a limousine to pick him up and bring him to the White House.'

"When he arrived, he was taken to a small room on the lower level, where the President, the Director of the CIA, and a couple of Generals were waiting for him. There was a bottle of champagne chilling in a bucket of ice on the table. The President shook his hand and began telling him how happy he was that they would be working together. The champagne was opened and a glass of it was handed to him. He sipped from it, as he was led around the room and introduced to the others. What he did not know was that his glass had been treated with a very potent drug. Ten minutes after taking his first sip, he passed out.'

'They kept him sedated and took him to a psychiatric hospital that was run by the CIA. Using truth drugs, they questioned him, and learned that there was a whole group of people like him. They believed that this group recruited and somehow trained people to use these abilities. They asked him over and over again where the headquarters of this group was located. When he told them that it was in another plane of existence, they became very agitated. They were beginning to ask for the names of others in the group, when some of our people found him. They transported him physically out of the hospital to the home of one of his friends, where he was allowed to sleep off the drugs. Since that day, the government has been frantically searching for us and, of course, what one government knows they all know rather quickly.'

'That is why as soon as someone starts going through the change, we send someone to explain things to them. Any one of the spectacular stunts you pulled, when you first started changing would have been enough to get the attention of these agents. Luckily, you never did anything that they could trace back to you. Thank God, you never materialized in front of anyone, before I could get to you."

"How do you know when someone is about to go through the change," I asked?

"In the early stages of the change, a person gives off something like a psychic homing beacon. There is a group called the Searchers that, among other things, monitors the entire planet for these psychic signals. When they are detected, one of us is notified and we begin to watch over that person until the change is complete. That person is then contacted and everything is explained to them, as I am doing for you now."

I thought about this for a while and then said, "Surely these government agents can't be much of a threat to us. With the powers we have, what can they do that we can't counter?"

"If we are able to get into the spirit form, they can't touch us. We have an automatic defense mechanism that takes over as we leave the body. An invisible barrier is formed that nothing, short of a nuclear blast, can penetrate. The danger comes in them sneaking up on us and knocking us unconscious. Once that happens, they can keep us drugged, which keeps us trapped in our bodies. In this state, they can get a lot of information from one of us that could put others at risk as well. They can also kill a body, which they have in such a state."

"That brings up a good question. What happens if we are killed, or if we just die of natural causes? I assume that once we have gone through the change, then this alters the normal reincarnation cycle."

"Yes," she said, "it does. Once you die, you have a choice. You can stay on this plane for a while, limited to spirit form only, or you can become a member of the Searchers. However, your days of experiencing the joys of physical existence on this plane are ended once you die."

"How many people go through the change each year?"

"Not many! I would estimate it to be no more than one or two a year. Some years, there may be none at all."

"If there is no more than one or two a year, that certainly does not seem to be enough to keep almost a thousand of us busy searching for them. There must more to it than that."

She gave me one of those measuring looks of her's and seemed suddenly very serious.

"You are right, of course. This is the part I have been a little hesitant to talk about, mainly because it is so difficult to believe at first. The Searchers are part of a much larger group of people, with varied skill levels and responsibilities. This group is, in many ways, responsible not only for this planet, but the entire galaxy. Earth is not the only planet in the galaxy where intelligent life exists. There are also many other planes of existence. As I mentioned before, there are some beings that could wipe out an entire world with no more effort than we use to swat a fly.'

'Someone must watch out for and guide the worlds that contain life, and are unaware of the dangers that exist in the universe, until they are able to protect themselves. The Searchers are one part of a school that trains us for this purpose. It also contains groups known as the Protectors and the Teachers. The whole organization is affectionately known as Godhood School."

I started to laugh, but I suddenly had a really weird feeling about this, and the laugh died in my throat. I swallowed and said, "And what is the ultimate goal for a graduate of Godhood School?"

She gave me a kind of worried smile, took a deep breath and said, "To become the God of an entire world."

4.

<u>Things are never</u>
<u>what they seem.</u>
<u>Ignorance is bliss,</u>
<u>but only knowledge</u>
<u>can set you free.</u>
The Book of Life

I stood looking down on the city lights again, floating at about ten thousand feet. I had been doing this a lot lately. It seemed to help me think. Laura had been good about giving me some space since our first conversation about Godhood school. It was not that I was trying to avoid her or that I was upset with her, but it takes a while to come to grips with this. I could imagine myself doing a lot of different things, but being a god was not one of them. It was one thing to have strange new powers and to play games with them, but it was something altogether different to be responsible for a whole planet of beings.

I had found out that no one was forced into this position. I could stay in another area as a Searcher, Protector, or Teacher, as long as I wanted to. Any of these positions had great appeal and responsibility, but they were not intended to be permanent. They are a training ground for the final goal of the ultimate trainer and protector. The problem was, I had already been approached and told that I had been selected for accelerated training, as soon as I was willing to start. It seemed that someone thought I was a good candidate for Supreme Being of a young world, about 35 light years from Earth. As I looked back on my life, with all the mistakes and ill feelings towards others, I simply could not see myself as an example of virtue or holiness. I would not make a good Pope, much less God.

I was ready to procrastinate for a couple of centuries, at least. Someone must have made a mistake. Who knew enough about me to decide what I was or was not capable of? Why the rush? Surely, someone had me mixed up with someone else. I would go through some training. I would help search for others going through the change. I would go through some more training. Maybe I would help do some teaching. Then, go through some more training. Then, maybe, some time far in the future, I would be willing to discuss it again. Maybe, in time, my self image would change, but somehow, I could never see it changing that much. Fool on the hill? Maybe. Holy man? Perhaps, but less likely. God? Sorry, I just don't see it happening.

I thought back to my younger days as a child in Michigan. I remembered the Sunday School teachers pounding it into me that I was a sinner. We were all sinners and did not deserve to even live on God's beautiful Earth, much less ever be physically in His presence in Heaven. The dogma started diverging here, depending on which of the several Christian denominations, I had been involved in over the years, was being espoused. However, they all had one central theme. We, that is to say humans, are all dirty, vile, undeserving sinners, new born infants included. We are all going to burn in hell for eternity, no matter how hard we try to live a good life. Only belief in Jesus could stop this from happening. Unless we had been "Saved", nothing we ever did was good enough to get us off the "slime of the universe" list.

Of course, once saved, always saved; at least, according to the Baptists. So once you had accepted Christ into your heart, you could do just about anything, and still go to heaven when you died. The only difference being that you might have to live in the slums of Heaven, instead of a mansion. The Nazarenes believed that you could actually achieve spiritual perfection after being saved. They believed that the Holy Spirit would inhabit you and you would become incapable of any act that might be considered sinful. The Pentecostals believed that the Holy Spirit would inhabit and control you only on certain occasions. This could manifest itself as speaking in tongues, healing through the laying on of hands, and other assorted miracles.

Catholics believe that we are always in a state of sin, while we are on this earth. However, if you do penance (a nice word for punishment) as prescribed by a Priest, you will eventually reach

Heaven. You will, however, be required to spend some time in Purgatory to atone for all the sins you committed during your lifetime.

Jews have required Rituals that must be performed to make up for our general unclean condition. All religions require constant and unending prayer, sacrifice of one kind or another, adherence to certain rules and taboos and, in the end, it is never enough in one lifetime. In order to reach Heaven, Nirvana, the next plane of existence or whatever, we require either the intervention of a God, Saints, time in hell, or all of the above. After a lifetime of this, is it any wonder that I do not feel worthy of being God to a new race of beings?

The more I thought about this, the more confused I became. There was no way I was going to figure this one out on my own. Obviously, with every religion and every denomination of the same religion claiming that they had the one and only truth, they could not all be right. Yet, they all claimed that if you did not believe as they did, you were going to hell.

Who was right? Was there really one correct view and all others were wrong? Were there certain ones that were mostly right and only a little wrong? Were there others that were mostly wrong and only a little right? Did every one have a little kernel of truth and not much more? Is there a Heaven? Is there a hell? Is there really only one God who created everything, or are there many Gods, as man believed before the Judaic/Christian concept of religion spread over the world? Are we committing blasphemy by playing God, or is this the way it has always been? Was Jesus the real Son of the One God? I had to know! This was not something I could accept someone else's word on. I no longer had to. I was now able to travel back in time, and find out for myself.

The thought of this was chilling to me, to finally know! Did I really want to know the truth? What if I did not like what I found out? What if I could not live up to what was really required of me? It is one thing to say I believe this or that, knowing that you are guessing at best. It kind of gives you a safety cushion for the afterlife. If you are wrong, you think you can use ignorance as an excuse, and maybe talk your way out of paying for your sins. But to know, to really know, *the* truth that takes away all excuses. Knowledge brings with it responsibility.

Oh man, how did I get here? I only wanted to dream about flying! I find out I have all these wonderful powers, became independently wealthy, married the woman of my dreams, and then mess it all up by trying to unlock the secrets of the universe. It's like getting everything you ever wanted for Christmas, and then finding out that Santa Claus is not real. Not only that, but then you suddenly start getting the credit card bills and find out that you must pay for your own presents. Who in hell issued me this cosmic Visa anyway?

Try as I might, I could not talk myself out of this. I had to get some answers. There were just too many ethical questions here that must be settled before I could decide what to do next. I headed back home to talk to Laura. I wanted to get this settled right away, but I also wanted to explain what I planned to do and get her feedback. She had a really good grasp of how my mind worked and talking to her often helped me see flaws in my own logic that I had not noticed before. I also wanted to ask her if she was interested in going with me. Maybe she had already made this same journey.

I flew slowly back toward our new home in Colorado. We had bought a nice little three bedroom ranch style home on 120 acres of land, just about one mile from a state park. The view was magnificent. The mountains were everywhere and our property was mostly wooded. In fact, the driveway from the road to our house twisted and turned through the trees so much, you could not see the house until you were practically in the garage. There was a small stream that started up in the mountains and ran very rapidly downhill and passed about 25 yards behind the house. The sound that it made was a lullaby that sang us to sleep every night. We fell in love with it on sight.

There was a lot of wildlife on and around our property. I had discovered that I could sense their presence and actually communicate with them after a fashion. It was not the same as the mental communication with others of my own kind that Laura had taught me to do. That was like talking to each other, but without making any sound. The communication with animals was on a much more subtle level. It was mostly emotions such as fear, hunger, love, and loneliness.

Yes, some animals do indeed get lonely. Some animals, I found out later, can express much more complex and abstract ideas. Gorillas, chimps, and dolphins come very close to human communication, if you know how to listen. They are positively overjoyed when they find a human that can hear them. In fact, one of the most gentle and loving beings that I have ever met, is an old silver back Gorilla, whose name translates as "Sees Too Much."

Laura was shocked that I could do this. It was not something she had ever been able to do. She could sense an animal's presence, but she had never been able to communicate with them. I have been working with her on this and she is making good progress. She tells me that this is one of the reasons that I was selected for accelerated training. It is not that this was something new. There are others who can communicate with animals, but it is usually a skill that is developed only after years of training. I wondered what they would think if I told them that I can feel the lives of an entire city of people all at once.

We had been flying over the Himalayan mountains, one

evening, and I was wondering what the Tibetan people were like. What must it be like to live their life? Suddenly, I started at the taste and smell of a meat I had never experienced before. At the same time, I was aware of conversation going on around me in a language that was both foreign and familiar to me at the same time. I was so startled that I immediately broke the contact. I had momentarily tuned in to someone having supper in the village we were flying over.

I stopped and hovered over the small town and gradually reached out again, only this time, not to an individual. I just opened myself to the feelings emanating from below me. I found that I could either get the general feel of the whole town or, like fine tuning a radio, hear individual thoughts, and finally actually enter the mind and body of one person. This was something else that I was not supposed to be able to do yet. It was a skill that was taught in Protector training, according to Laura, and was supposed to be very difficult. Entering into a person's mind, while in close physical proximity, is one of the early skills we develop after the change. Doing it from a distance and feeling the thoughts or emotions of more than one person at a time was supposed to be a skill that took years to develop.

Since that first time, I had been practicing it a lot. Hovering over a city the size of Phoenix, with millions of lives unrolling beneath you, is staggering the first time you do it. The emotions rising up over you are enough to make you wonder how anyone can live in all that and not be conscious of it. The rage, the hate, the violence, the love, the loneliness, the births, the deaths, the fulfillment, the emptiness, and the constant cry of, "I need!", is almost too much to bear. I could only take it for short periods of time. It tended to make me feel as if the life was being sucked right out of me. I never realized how much emotional need there is in the human race.

You would think that being able to see all of the dark things that others hide inside, would cause you to view them with disgust and revulsion. This is simply not so. The more you know about how a person's mind really works, not the image they try to project, but the real person, the more you realize how alike we all are. How frail is the human ego! How easily hurt we all are, and how long it takes to heal that hurt.

Those who cry the loudest about the sins of others are the ones who are most afraid of what they find inside themselves. We try to make ourselves feel better about our own shortcomings by demanding that others live up to our publicly held ideas of right and wrong. Then we secretly pray that no one ever finds out about our own transgressions. Our fear makes us mean spirited and spiteful, and we do not understand how much we hurt those around us.

In the Bible, Adam and Eve's son Cain was so jealous of his

brother that he finally murdered him and hid the body. When God asked him where his brother Able was, Cain answered, "Am I my brother's keeper?" In the end, Cain's inability to understand his brother's true feelings and motives, or even his own, caused his brother's death, and caused him to be cursed by God. If we all had to feel what those around us were feeling, then we would know that the answer to the question, "Am I my brother's keeper?" is yes. That is, unless you enjoy feeling your brother's pain along with your own.

I returned home and starting trying to explain to Laura what I had in mind. She listened quietly, until I was finished. When I asked her if she wanted to join me on my time trip, she said, "No, I don't think I should. This is a thing you need to do alone, since it involves your own beliefs and view of the world. I don't think you need someone else to intrude and color the experience, even accidentally, with their own pre-conceived ideas. Besides, I'm not sure I am ready to do this yet. When it is my time, I will go on my own quest for truth."

As usual, she understood, and knew instinctively what was right for me. I don't think I have ever met a less selfish person. I could tell that she was concerned about the way I had been behaving lately. She knew that I was having a hard time dealing with the direction some wanted my life to take. We were still newlyweds and were still discovering the joys of being together. What I most wanted was about another 50 years or so with Laura, and no responsibilities.

I needed time for healing, and the simple joys of being alive. Although no one could force us to do anything, I was getting some pressure from the Protectors to start Godhood School, as soon as possible. They appear to be good people and I trust their motives, but I still have some things to resolve, and I still resent being pushed. So, this trip will help clear up a lot of questions that I still have, and may also help delay making the decision, which I will soon have to make. At least, I should soon have a lot more facts to help make the right choice.

So, I kissed Laura, went into the bedroom, lay down on the bed, closed my eyes, and left my body again. Since no one was exactly sure of the dates things in the Bible had happened, I had to estimate and experiment to find the time that I was looking for. After popping out in several different times and places, I finally located the one I had been looking for. It was about two o'clock in the morning and there was a large number of people sleeping in an area next to what I believed was the Sea of Galilee. Apart from these people was a smaller group of about a dozen men, also sleeping. I chose one of them and entered his sleeping mind. James, his name was James.

"James, where is he? Where did he go?" I nudged his mind just enough to cause him to respond, as if to a dream.

"East. He headed east out into the wilderness alone."

I left him there to fall back asleep almost instantaneously, and headed east. I sent out a questing thought to try to locate a life force in the area ahead of me. I felt someone not too far away up in the hills. I followed the tenuous trail, until I saw a man sitting on a rock, staring off towards Jerusalem. The moon was almost full and it was a nearly cloudless night. I could see him pretty clearly. He was about my height or maybe a little taller. He was lean, but not skinny and had shoulder length hair. He was sitting so still, I thought he might be asleep. I glided around to his right and in front of him to get a better look. It was then that I saw that his eyes were open.

Was this him? Had I found the person I was looking for? He certainly didn't look very much like any of the paintings I had seen. I was about ready to reach out to his mind to find out who he was, when he smiled and looked directly at me.

"That won't be necessary," he said. "I am the man they call Jesus, and I have been expecting you."

5.

<u>Loving another</u>
<u>makes you worthy of</u>
<u>being loved.</u>
The Book of Life

As Laura walked into the bedroom, she saw her husband lying there on the bed, looking for all the world like a sleeping little boy. She walked over and lay down next to him with her head on his chest. She took every opportunity these days to be close to him. "Poor guy!" she thought. "He has been through a lot lately, and there is much more to come. He's getting a lot of pressure to start training and he feels that he is not ready yet. He does not feel worthy. In fact, he doesn't seem to feel worthy of anything, except the scorn that seems to have been heaped upon him his whole life.'

'I love him! Not just a little, not with part of my heart, or even most of my heart, but completely! I have loved him for some time now. He still does not know how long I watched him, before we actually met, and how much I know about him. My brother Danny almost let the cat out of the bag, when they first met. Damn him! He did it just to watch me blush."

It was about a year ago that Laura had been approached by one of the Protectors. He had told her that there was a man who was in the very early stages of the change, and he had thought Laura might be interested in this man. This was a pretty strange thing for a Protector to say, so Laura had asked him why she would be interested in this particular case. He had smiled and said, "It is the man, not the case, you would be interested in."

Laura had replied, "Oh really? Are you playing matchmaker now too? Being a Protector doesn't give you enough to do? What's going on?"

"Sorry, can't tell you. All I can say is that I have instructions, from a very highly placed personage, to tell you about this guy. I will take you to him the first time. Beyond that, all I am allowed to say is that it will be worth your time to get to know him."

Laura never could say no to a puzzle, so she let the Protector take her to where this person lived. As soon as he had gotten her there, he smiled, winked, and disappeared. This was too bizarre! Laura almost left without going inside, but, as she hovered there in front of the door to the man's apartment, her curiosity got the better of her, and she moved through the door, and into his living room.

What she saw was a slightly short man in his late forties, overweight and balding. He was not ugly, but neither was he what one would call attractive. He was sitting on the sofa watching television. She was about to leave and write the whole thing off as a bad joke on someone's part, when she noticed that he was crying. The tears were streaming from his eyes, and he was sobbing as he looked at the TV.

Laura looked and saw that he was watching an old Cary Grant movie called, "An Affair To Remember." It was the scene where Cary Grant is standing in the rain, at the top of the Empire State Building, waiting for Deborah Kerr, the woman he had been parted from for a year. The woman never showed up, because she had been hit by a car crossing the street, to keep their rendezvous, but he did not know this. He took the last elevator of the day down from the top, thinking that she had not come, because she no longer loved him.

Gently, Laura reached out and touched the mind of the man, who was watching the television. Waves of grief, loss, and unrequited love washed over her, like a tidal wave! The man had seen this movie a hundred times, and knew that they got together in the end, but it made no difference. He was caught up in a catharsis of monumental proportions. Laura pulled back in utter amazement! She had never experienced such an emotional outpouring from a man before. Someone was right; this was a person that may be well worth getting to know.

Laura had never had much luck with men. She had never been involved with a physically abusive individual, although she had known many women who have. She had, however, had plenty of personal experience with the macho, posturing, pretty boys that women often seem to find so attractive, when they are young. It doesn't take very many experiences, with this type of man, for a woman to learn that there is no room in his life, or his heart, for anyone but himself. She thought about the different types of men that she had known.

There are the rich and powerful men. To them, a woman is nothing but a possession. They are consumed by the drive to always take first place. Softness or tenderness has no place in their lives. They consider such things a weakness, and weakness is something they dare not show. They are generally willing to sacrifice anything, or anyone, to advance one step toward their goals. They can never reach a point in their lives, where they have enough.

Then there are the workaholics. They are very similar to the rich men, except that they claim that everything they are doing is for their woman. They are sacrificing their lives in order to get her the things that she wants and needs. Oh, they can be very generous indeed. They will give her anything she asks for, except their time. Marry this type of man, and you will spend the rest of your life alone.

The car enthusiasts are more concerned with a good paint job, than a good relationship. The sports fanatic's idea of romance is to have sex on the couch during half time. Attorneys think they're smarter than anyone else. Construction workers don't want a woman if she has an IQ above the freezing point of water. Jocks are so in love with their own bodies, they hardly notice that a woman has one. Even ministers will neglect their women, to see to the needs of their flocks. All in all, not a pretty picture, so when Laura found a man who was able to cry, even in private, over what is considered to be a "woman's movie", she was interested enough to want to learn more.

So, Laura began to follow him. She watched him at work as he tried to deal with the day to day grind, with a sense of humor. He seemed to have no trouble working with others. He was patient, gentle, and always ready to help. Even when someone was short or snippy with him, he seemed to have the ability to defuse the situation, and leave them smiling. There were several women he worked with that he obviously was interested in, but he never pushed. He would smile and talk with them, but Laura never saw him ask anyone for a date.

Laura started following him when he left work for the day. He almost always went straight home. He would stop at the grocery store once in a while, but that was about it. No trips to the bar, either alone or with friends from work. Laura wondered about this a lot. Why did he seem to choose to be alone all the time? He had one close friend that he talked to on the phone occasionally, but that seemed to be the extent of his social life. The rest of the time, he seemed to do not much more than watch television.

There was a picture of him and a woman on the wall in his living room. Laura wondered who she was. They looked good together, and they looked happy in the picture. Laura became so curious one day that she reached out and touched his thoughts. She nudged him carefully to look up at the picture. As his eyes focused on it, in a rush of thoughts and images, Laura got the answer to her question.

This was an old girlfriend that he had lived with for several years. It had been a good relationship in the beginning and they had been very much in love. This had been the first woman he had dated since his divorce several years earlier, and he was fiercely devoted to her. Unfortunately, this was not the case with her. This woman did love him, but not the way he needed. She had told him in the very beginning that no one would ever come before her family in her life. This included her parents and her two grown children, all of whom lived in another state, and her two sisters. He had understood this, but did not know that this also meant that he would always take second place in her life, not only to her family, but to her friends as well.

This woman had also warned him that she had been living alone for about five years, when they met, and she liked it. He now felt that he had been a total fool to believe that this could ever change. There had been enough times, when she seemed to have changed how she felt that he had been able to convince himself that there was hope. She had broken up with him three times, and had come back each time saying that she had learned how much she loved and needed him. Each time, he had swallowed his pride, silenced his common sense, and had taken her back. When she finally moved three thousand miles away, to stay with her pregnant daughter, all the while telling him she loved him and always would, he finally ended it.

The woman had called him and written him letters for months afterward, always talking about how much she missed him and how much she wanted to come back. When he finally called her bluff and suggested that she do what she had said she was tempted to do, sell everything and come back, she waffled. She said she should give it at least six months, before she just gave up and came back. Sensing that she would never change and knowing that he could no longer stand to be a poor second to people, who treated her like crap, he wished her a good life and asked her to never contact him again. It had been the hardest thing he had ever done.

This was becoming kind of scary for Laura, as she realized

that she was starting to really feel for this guy. She had made a promise to herself that she would never become involved with another man, and she had been quite serious about it. Yet, here she was following this guy around and poking into his life. Laura decided that she was not only breaking her promise to herself, but was also invading his privacy, so she made up her mind to just walk away and pretend that she had never met him. After all, if he was going through the change, they would eventually meet anyway.

Laura went back to her normal routine for a couple of days, when the same Protector, who had introduced her to the mystery man, showed up at the door. He was a tall, lean man, named Gregory, who always looked as if he were keeping a rather amusing secret. His long, light brown hair seemed to be perpetually falling across his face and over his eyes. This seemed to enhance a rather impish grin and made him seem, at times, like a little boy. This was very deceiving, since he was actually over 700 years old. He had been a Protector for approximately 600 of those years and had seen enough during that time to permanently depress any other person. Yet, he was somehow able to maintain his humorous approach to life.

Laura was not too sure exactly what Gregory's job encompassed. All she was certain of was that he worked for someone with a lot of authority. One must understand that not all of the work the protectors do is secret, but a good portion of it has to be. Much of their work deals with time lines stretching for hundreds, sometimes thousands of years. A single piece of seemingly insignificant information could have repercussions that could literally change major historical events.

It is true that all of those, who have been through the change, are capable of time travel. It is also true that, although they are taught not to make any major changes to history, without checking with the Protectors first, they can, and sometimes do, change the past. Laura had many a discussion with Protectors about this and it usually ended up being more confusing at the end of the discussion, than it was at the beginning. It went into the areas of free will vs. destiny, cause and effect, multiple time lines, wheels within wheels, plot and counter plot, and other such contradictory ideas. The major upshot of this was that the so called future is very fluid and subject to change.

Part of the job of the Protectors is to function almost as weavers creating a tapestry. That tapestry is the future of the human race, but it is not always woven to a pattern of their own design. They ultimately answer to one person on all matters that affect the future of the human race. That person is the one chosen as the "God" of that planet. No one, outside of a very few of the Protectors, even knows who this person is. No one is too sure whether this person is even human. It seemed most likely that they are not, since many humans have been recruited and trained to be the God of another planet, much as Laura's husband was now being recruited. That person has ultimate control over the major events of human history, and over any smaller pieces that they so desire. There is no court of appeal for one of their decisions. The Protectors are the ones that correct mistakes made by others and help nudge human history in the direction our God wishes it to take. One could also call them Angels.

Laura said to Gregory, "Ok, Gregory, what now? You got another blind date for me?"

Gregory smiled that boyish smile and looked down at her, in a way that reminded Laura of her brother, and said, "No, not exactly. I need you to come with me to the Protectorate for a little bit, if you don't mind. We have some information we feel you would benefit from."

"Information about what?"

"You'll find out when we get there," he said.

"Gregory, you know I don't like all this cloak and dagger nonsense. What's the big secret?"

"Sorry kid, but you know how this stuff works sometimes. All I can say is that it is very important. Of course, I certainly will not try to force you to come if you refuse. You know we don't operate that way, but I promise that you will feel it was worth the trip."

Laura thought about it for a minute. She was not actually afraid. She knew neither Gregory nor any member of the Protectorate would ever hurt anyone, but this was making her nervous. She had no doubt it was important, but the question was, important to whom? Laura had a weird feeling that it had something to do with the guy Gregory had taken her to see. On the one hand, she definitely did not like anyone trying to interfere in her personal business. On the other hand, the Protectorate did not meddle in anything that was not part of some master plan.

"Ok, I'll meet you there in about five minutes," she said. Gregory winked at her and faded out. Laura had been emptying the dishwasher, when Gregory showed up, so she finished putting the dishes away. Then she walked into the living room, sat down on the sofa, closed her eyes, and left her body. She took one last look around, gathered up her courage, and headed for the Protectorate.

When Laura arrived, she found Gregory standing in the main entrance way waiting for her. He took her arm and they started walking down a long hallway together. Laura looked at Gregory and said, "I still am not too thrilled about this."

Gregory smiled down at her and said, "Don't worry. The Governor could still call with a stay of execution, before we throw the switch." They were still laughing as they walked into a room where about ten others waited for them.

Gregory escorted her to a seat, squeezed her hand, and walked out. Laura looked at the people in the room with her. There were six women and four men, of which she only knew one by name. Laura looked around the room quickly. It was just large enough to accommodate all of them without seeming crowded. There were a couple of sofas and several easy chairs spread around the room, as well as a couple of small tables. The floor was covered with a deep pile carpet that had the feel of luxury about it. The walls seemed to be covered in oak paneling and had several pictures hanging on them. The overall feel of the room was one of comfort and security.

Laura looked at the one person whom she knew, and said, "Okay, Michael, what's so important?"

They all found seats and turned to face her. Michael smiled and said, "So, what do you think of the man, Gregory introduced you to?"

"I knew it! I just knew it!" Laura thought, but said,

"Why?"

"I believe Gregory told you that he was in the early stages of the change. He will soon be in the position of needing an advisor to help him make the transition as easy as possible, and to help keep him out of danger for a while. How would you like to be that advisor?"

"Why me?"

"Why not you?"

Laura opened her mouth to reply, couldn't think of an answer that made any sense, and closed it again. "Why not me?" She thought about it, and found that she really did not have a good answer. She was well aware that someone going through the change needed help. It had not been very long ago that she had gone through the same thing. It was not an easy adjustment under the best of circumstances, and she had been very appreciative of all the help her advisor had given her. Here was an opportunity for Laura to give something back by helping another. Why was she hesitating?

"There is something missing here! You are not telling me everything. Why have I been summoned to the Protectorate, to a meeting with ten Protectors, to be asked to do this job? This is not normal procedure. If this were anyone else, Gregory would simply have asked me to do it. What makes this guy so special?"

They all looked at each other, as if for moral support for a moment, and then turned back to Laura. Michael seemed to have been elected spokesperson for the group, because it was he who responded.

"As you are well aware, Laura, we cannot always give people all the information they would like. This may be one of those times. We can tell you that this person is indeed a special case. Just why this is so, we are not free to divulge at this time. Let's concentrate for the moment on what we can tell you.'

"This man is in the very early stages of the change. He is exhibiting all the classic signs, plus a few that are not so typical. His life has been followed very closely. There have been a lot of hard things happening to him all his life. Some of them happened naturally. Many of them were, well, let us say arranged. He has been pushed, prodded, and sometimes dragged kicking and screaming down a certain path in his life. It is a testament to his abilities that even before he started going through the change, he was marginally aware of this. It has made him very difficult to influence. He is very strong willed and has a lifelong distaste for authority figures."

"He likes people, but does not trust them very much. He is very generous, if it is his idea, but will give no help to anyone who demands it. Despite the abysmal luck he has had with all women in his life, from his mother on up; he is a very gentle man, who still believes in true love. He is a very patient man, but has little or no patience with those who deliberately hurt another in order to gain money, power, or prestige for themselves. He has a great capacity for love, but has been denied the return of this love to him his whole life."

Laura stopped him there and said, "You're telling me that this man's life has been controlled to a certain extent, in order to further someone's plans for him. Whose plans? Who has been doing this to him, and why, and again, what has any of this got to do with me?"

Michael smiled at Laura and said, "In many ways, you are much like him. Why are we paying so much attention to this man? We have been ordered to."

Laura opened her mouth to ask another question, but Michael held up his hand and said, "I know, I know, ordered to by whom? By the Boss!"

Their boss??? With a catch in her voice, Laura asked, "Which Boss, exactly?"

With no hint of a smile, Michael looked her in the eye, and

spoke one word.

"Him!"

"By Him, you mean the big Boss? The guy with no name?"

"Oh, He has a name! In fact, He has several. We've just never been really sure which one, if any, is correct."

It always amazed Laura how certain words could sound capitalized, but when talking about Him, it actually worked. She was not really afraid of Him, and she certainly was not religious, but this guy had complete control of the planet for thousands of years. That kind of power and commitment did deserve some respect. They gave Laura a little time to absorb this bit of information, and then Michael continued.

"As to what all this has to do with you, again, this man needs an advisor. The boss would like it to be you. You may refuse if you wish, but we do need an answer now. If you agree, then there is some further information you will need. If you are not interested, please feel free to leave now."

Laura sat there with all of them staring at her expectantly, for a moment. She had one last question.

"If I accept, will you then tell me why it is so important that I be the advisor, instead of someone else?"

Michael laughed out loud. "You really are a most stubborn young woman. No, we cannot tell you that. However, I can say that if you take the assignment, it will all become clear to you in the near future. So, what do you say?"

Laura took a deep breath, smiled, and said, "Okay, I'll do it."

They all smiled at Laura and the tension, which she had hardly been aware of, seemed to dissipate immediately. Michael walked over, shook her hand and said, "You will not regret the decision you made here today, I promise you. As I said, there is some further information, which we are instructed to give you. In order to give it to you as quickly as possible and so that you will have no trouble remembering it, we will mind link with you. Please, make yourself comfortable and we will begin."

Mind linking is a telepathic joining of minds in order to pass a lot of information quickly. It can be done between as few as two people, but can include many more. Laura sat back in her seat and closed her eyes. She reached out to the others in the room and felt them respond. She relaxed and let them take over.

What took place then was a trip through part of the life of the man, to whom Laura was about to become advisor. Memories that seemed to be his were fed into Laura quickly. They started at a very early age and seemed to skip back and forth. It was all happening so quickly that she did not have time to absorb every detail. That would come later after it was all over and Laura's mind had a chance to catch up. She received years of his memories in what seemed to be no more than minutes to Laura. She began to see what Michael had meant about the hard things that had happened to this man. His life had been difficult in the extreme. By the time it was over, Laura found herself crying.

Laura felt the others, in the room, reach out and mentally hug her. They held her for a while in this manner, until she had regained control of her emotions and did not feel so alone. Laura opened her eyes and looked at them.

"How does he stand it? I never felt so alone. I've watched him and he seems to cope quite well. How does he do it?"

"What we have given you is only a piece, a small piece, of his life. The Boss felt it would be easier for you to help him through the change, if you knew something of what he has gone through. This is a very complicated man and one in which the boss has an uncommon interest. We do not know why yet ourselves, but we feel that it will become clear to us all in the not too distant future. As for you, there were a lot of others the boss could have chosen as this guy's advisor, but He insisted on you. You can bet there is a damn good reason why. We are sure that it will be beneficial to you both. Thank you for your help, and we will be in touch."

Laura went back home and fixed herself a cup of tea. As she sat there sipping the tea and staring out of the window, she had time for the memories, which she had been given, to coalesce and arrange themselves in some kind of order. She reviewed them over and over again. This man had spent most of his life trying to understand what he had been doing wrong, which kept anyone from loving and accepting him.

The truth was that he had done nothing wrong. Yet life had dealt him one cruel blow after another. From parents that could not say, "I love you." to an abusive father whom he could never please, and a mother who hated all men, to a string of girlfriends and finally a wife, who considered him nothing more than a walking wallet; this man had been through it. Failure after failure in love, business, personal relationships, overweight, early loss of his hair, the early death of one of his few true friends in an auto accident, a fire that burned all his personal possessions, except the clothes on his back, on and on.

The most amazing thing to Laura, though, was the fact that he got up every morning and started over again. He was bitter occasionally, but did not dwell on it. He was terribly lonely, but did not let it destroy him. Through it all he somehow retained a sense of humor. She had watched him at work and had wondered sometimes why he so often acted like a standup comic, looking for a job. It was his defense mechanism. It was how he dealt with the pressure. Both laughter and crying are great safety valves and can help one deal with all the crap the world can throw at us. Laughter is just more acceptable in public, especially for a man.

As Laura sat there and thought about him, she could not help herself. She left her body and found herself at his door. She found him asleep on the sofa and gently inserted herself into his sleeping mind. He was dreaming that he was lost in a very large and dark forest. Try as he might, he could not find his way out and there was no one there to help him. He finally gave up and sat down on the ground under a tree, with his arms wrapped around his knees, rocking back and forth, repeating over and over, "Alone!"

Something in Laura snapped and she inserted her image into his dream. She took him in her arms and held him like a child. Laura looked down at him and said, "No, not alone. Never alone!"

He looked at her and smiled, and the dream ended. Laura looked at him laying, there with that smile still on his face, and wondered why in the name of god she had done that. It shocked her so badly that she instantly popped back home and into her body. Laura sat up and rubbed her eyes, as if she had been asleep all night.

Why had she done that? Laura stood up and began to pace back and forth, trying to think it through. It must have been because of the mind linking. That must have caused her to be overly emotional or something. The last thing she needed was to become emotionally involved with this guy. Why did this little voice in the back of her head keep repeating, "Too late!"

Gradually, Laura's thoughts drifted back to the present moment. She looked at her beloved again, on the bed next to her, and gently touched his cheek. Since that incident with the dream, Laura had followed him and watched him. He may not have known it consciously, but she had been true to her word. He had never been truly alone since then. It did not take Laura long after that day, to admit to herself that she was hopelessly in love with him. She continued to be with him in his dreams, since she could not yet be with him in reality, right up to the time he started leaving his body at night. It had become clearer to her why the Boss was so interested in him, but that no longer mattered to her as much as it once had. She was happy for now just to be with him. For the first time in her life, she was content.

6.

There is no Truth,
only belief.
Therefore, be very
careful what you
believe.
The Book of Life

My heart was hammering away, as I stood there looking into the eyes of the man that a large portion of humanity has believed to be the Son of the living God, for almost two thousand years. He was smiling at me, as if he knew me. That made me a little nervous. He had said that he had been expecting me, and that made me even more nervous. He appeared to be waiting for me to say something, and that was why I had come here, but how do you ask Jesus about his divinity? Now that I was faced with the opportunity to finally get some answers, I was afraid to ask.

Oh sure, sitting there safe and secure in your own little world, where you are in control, it is easy to think you would not be nervous. Not so, my friend, believe me. Think about having a conversation with your priest, minister, or rabbi about sex, and tell me that it would not make you sweat a little. Now, imagine you are standing right in front of God, and you want to ask Him about right and wrong, heaven and hell. Under those circumstances, almost anyone would be lucky to get out any words at all other than, "Please don't hurt me."

He was still smiling at me, as if he knew how nervous I was, and wanted to put me at ease. He said, "Come now, don't be shy. I know you didn't travel 2,000 years into the past to just stand and look at me. We have more in common than you know, and it is not often that I have a chance to talk to one such as you these days. What can I do for you?"

Okay, I guess the best way to start is at the beginning. Gathering up all my courage, I smiled back at him and said, "Yes, I do have many things to ask you, and I guess the best way to start is just to ask it straight out. Are you the Son of God?"

He laughed quietly and said, "No, I am God. The one and only God of the planet you call Earth. Does that help you?"

I kind of shook my head and asked, "The God of Earth, not the God of all creation?"

He looked absolutely pained and said, "Oh my, no! God of Earth is more than enough. No one I know of can handle more than one world at a time. Let me make this easier for both of us. We, you and I, are the same. I am what you will soon become. You do not owe me any worship. Does that help?"

My head was spinning and I was having trouble concentrating. Struggling for some kind of hold on reality, or at least what I had always considered to be reality, I was not making the connection.

"What do you mean, we are the same?"

He sighed and looked back toward Jerusalem again. His voice was quiet and subdued, as he began talking to me.

"Many tens of thousands of your years ago, I was born into my last incarnation, as a flesh and blood being. Like you, I went through the change and was eventually recruited for our version of Godhood School. I was told that there was a world on the edge of what you call the Milky Way Galaxy that had a group of beings on it, who were starting to show promise. They would soon need a God to guide them and help them reach their eventual potential as a race. The world was called Earth. I was offered the job and soon accepted it."

"I say it again; you and I are more alike than you might believe. I too have a rather rebellious nature. I was convinced that I could do a better job, if I followed my own heart on certain things, rather than doing it the way I had been taught. After all, there really are no rules for this job. If there are, it is only because we have imposed them upon ourselves. It is pretty much a game of trial and error. Somehow, because of the very nature of beings such as you and me, we tend to make few true mistakes in the long run. We can correct and retry in the early stages of the development of our charges, without too much trouble. By the time they are more sophisticated, we are even more so."

I walked over and sat down on the ground facing him. I was beginning to come out of my initial shock at the things I was hearing. This was a priceless opportunity and I fully intended to get all I could from it, but so many questions! Where do I start?

"You are telling me that you are from another world. Yet, you look just like a human. How can this be? Is all sentient life in the universe human?"

"No, it is not. Neither am I truly human. I maintain this appearance, when I am manifesting myself on your planet, for obvious reasons. You will someday use the same trick for the benefit of the beings entrusted to your care."

"You talk as if I had already decided to accept this job, which everyone seems so intent on forcing on me. I am still very much undecided. What do you know about all of this? Whose bright idea was it to offer me this position anyway? Why is everyone so positive I am capable of handling something this important? I seem to be the only one who doesn't feel like I deserve such trust."

"That is as it should be. Anyone who is not daunted by the prospect of being responsible for the development of an entire planet of intelligent beings will never be in that position. The others feel that you are right for the job, because they have come to trust my judgment in such matters."

My mouth was hanging open by now and I'm sure my eyes were popping out as well. I must have looked like a total idiot, because he actually began to laugh. Not quietly like he had been earlier, but a loud, hearty, belly laugh. He was still laughing and wiping tears from his eyes as he said, "Oh, thank you! I really needed a good laugh right now. There has not been much worth laughing about in my life for a while."

I closed my mouth and looked at him for a moment, then opened it again, couldn't quite force any words out yet, and closed it again. I repeated this process several times, while he just sat there laughing at me. I was finally able to pull myself together enough to say, "Trust your judgment? You mean ...you ... this was ... you chose me for this?"

After a new round of laughter at my stammering response, he

finally stood, walked over, and put his arm around my shoulder and said, "Yes, it was my bright idea," and started laughing again. By this time, I must have become so surprised and confused that my old defense mechanism just kicked in and took over. I too began to laugh. What a sight this would have made if anyone had been around to see it. One God and one future God, under a starlit sky, in the middle of a desert, holding on to each other, and laughing as if they had both lost their minds. The shortest verse in the Bible is, "Jesus wept." I guess it had never occurred to me before this night that he might also have a sense of humor.

We walked over and sat down on the sand together. Gradually we got ourselves back under control and I started asking some of the other things that I had been wondering about. The laughter had released the last of the tension. I was no longer afraid of him or of what he might say.

"Okay, so the traditional religious beliefs of our world are not exactly on the mark. So is any of the stuff in the Bible or the Koran correct?"

"Some of it is fairly accurate historical fact. Most of it is not. Most of the stories in your Bible were not intended to be taken literally. There was a message in them and lessons of behavior to be learned, but then religion is always 99% man- made. You will find this out soon enough yourself. Try to teach a lesson without someone either twisting everything you say for their advantage, or taking every word to heart."

"Take these men that follow me around right now, calling themselves my apostles. I talk to them, but they do not really hear me. I say to them, these are stories, used to make a point. So, what do they do? Being human, they repeat the stories to others and represent them as actual occurrences. The worst part is that they do this deliberately. They know what I said. Yet, such underdeveloped beings feel that they must make things seem more mystical, if they are to impress their friends and neighbors. This is the way of men. I wish that it could be otherwise, but religion is a necessary evil."

"So this is the reason for the Jesus of Nazareth myth?"

"Yes. I have tried other things in the past and this is the only thing that works with such undeveloped souls. If there is no great and mysterious force in their lives that will both punish them for transgressions, and reward them for right thinking, their technology develops faster than their humanity, and they end up destroying their world."

He looked at me out of the corner of his eye and said, "You know, I have not enjoyed myself so much in quite a while. The people of your planet are a curious mixture of so many things. You have such a capacity for love and laughter, even at times of great stress and sorrow. Yet you take yourselves so seriously sometimes that it is difficult to believe there is any humor in you at all. It is your unpredictability that makes you so unique."

"I have need of an unpredictable wit for a time, to give me a fresh perspective and to lighten my load. So, will you travel with me for a while? It could be very instructive for you, and I could certainly use the company and moral support. What do you say?"

How could I say no to such a request? He was right; it would be a great opportunity for me. He had been in this God Game a long time and I would be a fool not to learn all I could from him. Besides, I liked him! He made me laugh, which was always a plus in my book. At the same time, there was something about him that made me want to protect him. He was somehow very vulnerable and lonely. If I could help him get through what was soon to come, then I would be most willing to do so.

I reached out and shook his hand and said, "Yes, thank you! I will stay with you for a while."

We stayed up the entire night talking. He told me of his home world and his people. He talked of his younger days and the dreams he had for his life before the change came and altered his future forever. He talked of his mate, whom he had little time to spend with, but loved profoundly.

He began to talk of the current political situation in this part of the world. Make no mistake; politics and religion go hand in hand. Power is present in both, and where there is power, there is contention. The Romans had conquered this entire area and ruled it with an iron hand. However, this part of the world was not really much to the liking of most Romans. It was too hot, too dry, and the people were rebellious. Most Roman Governors were fond of the pleasures of life and did not enjoy being involved in the petty grievances of merchants and thieves on a daily basis.

The Jewish religious leaders, however, thrived on such matters. They had been doing so for most of their history. So a deal was struck. The roman ruler allowed the Jewish religious leaders to continue to dispense their own brand of justice, as long as it involved only Jews and only Jewish law. This left him free to pursue his own pleasures most of the time and gave him a specific group of Jews to blame, and punish if things did not go the way he wished. It made the high ranking Jews feel less like slaves and gave them a real reason to make sure the Romans got what they wanted. It also made the average Jewish citizen feel as if Rome were granting them some small amount of independence.

So, the Roman Governor was happy, or as happy as he could be while he was away from Rome. The Jewish religious leaders were happy because they continued to maintain control over their people, even after being conquered. The only ones not happy were the poor people, who now had two sets of masters instead of one, but they did have their religion, which promised them the Messiah.

Yes, the Savior! The new leader that was promised, who would ease all their burdens, throw off the yolk of oppression, bring freedom, and restore the glory of Israel! He would come soon, and bring with him the power of the old "God With No Name." They knew this because their religious leaders told them so. Of course, the coming of the Messiah had been prophesied long ago with no result as yet, but when one is at the bottom of the political food chain, any hope is better than none.

The Romans were aware of the prophecy regarding the Messiah, of course. They made it their business to know such things. In many respects it is easier to conquer than it is to rule. The first requires brute force only. The second requires knowledge and finesse. It is certain that brute force was also used to rule at times, but that is expensive. An empire the size of Rome's could not be maintained, if they had to keep thousands of troops in every city, town, and village that they conquered. So Roman Governors were most often more politician than soldier.

Being politicians, they recognized another politician rather quickly, even in another culture. Rome had long known the value of religion in keeping a population under control. The Pharisees were masters of this game, so it should come as no surprise that the Roman Governor made full use of them to help control the rebellious inhabitants of Jerusalem. As long as no one tried to step forward as this Messiah and actually change anything, it was a useful tool. If that should ever happen, the Pharisees stood to lose much more than the Romans, and they knew it.

Now, add into this careful balancing act a young man, who not only preached love and equality, but also performed miracles. Here was a man who actually demonstrated, repeatedly, the power that the religious leaders claimed, but could not produce. Here was a man, who not only did not respect the rank of the powerful, but actually seemed to enjoy the company of the poor and powerless. Finally, add in the fact that the word Messiah was being used more and more often in relation to this man, and the powder keg was almost ready to blow.

Attempts were made to bring him into the fold, so to speak. They offered him a place in their ranks, if he would only play the game. They offered him power and money, if he would just stop performing miracles without their consent. They offered him fame as a teacher, if he would only teach their doctrine rather than this drivel about equality and brotherhood. They even offered him many beautiful young wives, if he would just stop rocking the boat. When he refused their attempts at bribery, it only convinced them that he must be mad as well as dangerous. After all, what sane man would turn down such offers?

They followed him from town to town becoming more and more angry, with each refusal. I stayed with him night and day and was aware of each offer. At one point, one of his adversaries said, "If you are of God, then let him give us a sign that we might believe."

This had been suggested many times in the past, but we all knew that nothing would ever convince them that they were wrong. This was wearing a little thin on me by now, so I decided to give this latest posturing Pharisee his wish. The words were no more than out of his mouth, when a whipped cream pie materialized out of thin air, flew straight into his face, and splattered everyone standing close to him. A complete and total hush fell over the watching crowd for a moment. Then he could stand it no longer, Jesus laughed!

No, laughed is too mild a word. With tears streaming from his eyes, he roared with laughter, until he could no longer stand. He fell to the ground, hugging his sides as spasm after spasm of laughter washed over him. At first, the crowd stared at him in amazement and could do or say nothing. Gradually, they too began to laugh. Soon, everyone in sight was laughing uncontrollably; everyone, that is, except the Pharisees. No trace of humor could be found on any of their faces, only fear and anger!

When he could control himself enough to talk coherently

again, Jesus stood up and faced the man hit with the pie and said, "So, my friend. Will that suffice? Do you now believe, or do you require more proof?"

The man ducked, as if he expected another pie. When none appeared to be forthcoming, he puffed himself up to his full height and said, "Do I believe that God threw a pie in my face? I should say not! If I find the person who threw that pie, we will make such an example of them that no one will ever dare to so disrespect one of us again. You will come to regret this day, this I promise you!"

Gathering what little remained of their dignity, the Pharisees stalked off to the Temple to report on this latest indictment of the young man from Galilee. As you are probably aware, this incident was never reported in any version of the biblical history of Jesus. I can only assume that it was believed that someone in the crowd threw the pie, even though many people saw it materialize. Perhaps they felt as the Pharisee did, that God would not stoop to throw a pie.

As we traveled, we grew to be good friends. I watched how he worked with the people and could see how much he cared for them. His patience was beyond anything I had ever witnessed. I saw him work with the apostles, trying to teach them about love and compassion. It was an uphill battle, always. He always saw the good in every situation and in every man. As we neared the city of Jerusalem and the culmination of his ministry, I was filled with a sense of dread. On the last night before we arrived, I could stand it no longer. He seemed happy and at ease until I blurted out, "You must know what awaits you in Jerusalem in the not too distant future. Do you really allow this to happen?"

His mood changed suddenly and he became very quiet. He nodded his head slowly and said, "The crucifixion must happen. Someone must provide them with an example of what love really means. They must begin to understand what they lose, when they allow other men to so rule their lives that an innocent can be slain for a belief. There is no one among them who will be willing to sacrifice their life for this cause, so the task falls to me. This is why your gift of laughter has meant so much to me at this time."

"But, you will not really allow them to physically hurt you, surely not! If this body is just a device for your use, you must be able to block out physical pain. You're not really here physically, only mentally, right?"

"You are right, but only up to a point. The body I currently wear is indeed a construct, but it is one that I have worn for over thirty years now. This period of the history of your planet has required my constant attention for most of that time, and this body has been very useful. I have grown fond of it, even though it has no existence apart from me. It is an extension of me, and in order for the crucifixion to be convincing, some pain must be allowed. I will not allow it to suffer as a true mortal would, but there will be pain."

"Yet, gladly would I suffer all of this, and more, if the most painful thing of all could be taken from me. Soon, all those who have followed me for years, have seen miracles and called themselves my friends, who profess undying love for me, all will deny even knowing me, and watch me die."

Never had I been so moved. I never even thought as I spoke. It just came out of my mouth, before I quite knew what I was saying.

"You do not have to do this. Let me do it for you."

Slowly, he reached out and touched my cheek. With tears in his eyes, he spoke, so quietly I could barely hear him.

"Ah, my friend, tell me now that you do not know why I chose you. You, and those like you, are the final result of what I do here and now. It would appear that I do excellent work!"

I laughed and hugged him to me. "Yes! Yes you do!" I wiped the tears from my eyes and said, "You made it sound earlier as if you had made some mistakes that had not been easy to correct. What would those be?"

"When this business in Jerusalem is over, ask me again."

Well, I guess most of you know the rest. I stayed with him, as he and the apostles marched into Jerusalem. The people lining the streets were all cheering him, and calling him Savior, and Messiah. Being there at that moment, it was hard to believe how soon these same people would be howling for his blood.

It was all playing out before me now, just as I had read about it so many times before. The last supper, Judas meeting with the Pharisees, the betrayal, the accusations, and the mock trial were all there. The Roman Governor really wanted to turn Jesus loose. He had no problem with him since his own spies had reported that Jesus did not preach revolt, and had never actually claimed to be this Messiah. He recognized the jealousy and envy the Pharisees had for this man.

The fact was, he actually enjoyed seeing this young man get the better of these old sharks, but they had stirred the people up to the point of riot. So in the end, he simply gave Jesus to them, and told them to try him under their own Jewish law. As he walked back into his palace, he cursed the Pharisees and all politicians in general. He knew he had in effect signed the man's death warrant.

"Damn these Jews! May they pay for this injustice for many generations to come?" This I heard him say with my own ears, as he walked away. I do not believe that he had any idea how prophetic this statement would be.

I watched as they beat him, and kicked him, and spat upon him. I cried out in anger and caused clouds to form above the city, and the wind to blow faster and faster. No one could see me but him; however, they certainly must have felt something out of the ordinary was going on. The soldiers were looking up at the skies and then at the Jewish priests. They were not happy about what was happening, but the blood lust in the Pharisees was near fever pitch. Nothing would stop them now.

I watched the apostles peeking out from behind buildings, and trying to lose themselves in the crowd; denying any knowledge of the man whom they had called Lord for years. Then, they began to drive nails into his wrists and feet!

The tears sprang from my eyes, as if a fountain had been opened. I screamed "NO" with each blow of the hammer, and matched each stroke with a bolt of lightning. Each thunderbolt came a little closer to the group of Pharisees and priests standing together. Jesus saw what was happening, looked at me and said, "Forgive them! They truly do not know what they do."

I stayed and waited with him for the end. I had whipped the storm up into such a frenzy that almost everyone had left to seek shelter. Only a few people, who were not afraid to admit their love for him, and a few soldiers remained. He looked down for his apostles and saw none. He cried out, "My students, my friends, why have you forsaken me?" Of course, when the bible was written this was changed to "My God, my God, why have you forsaken me?" This was because it was his former apostles writing, and they did not want to admit to anyone what he had actually said. It did not paint a very good picture of them after all.

Finally, he looked at me and said, "It is time, my friend. Let us end this."

I nodded and entered the body of one of the soldiers. I placed the command in his mind, withdrew and watched him lift up his spear. One clean thrust through the heart, and it was done. He withdrew from the body and stood next to me. He hugged me to him and said, "Thank you, my friend, for staying with me. You may never know how much it has meant to me. Now, you should be getting back home, don't you think? You have much to do and much to learn."

I nodded and said, "Yes, you are right. I do indeed have much to learn. Before I go, however, you promised to give me an example of one of the mistakes you had made in the beginning."

"I guess you deserve to hear about one anyway. I said that I use this human appearance for obvious reasons. It was not always so.

In the beginning of my time here, I decided that the teachers in Godhood School did not know everything. I saw no reason not to use my true appearance here on this planet. After all, I am a God. Why would I look just like them? I had not taken into account the total arrogance of the human species. Your ancestors firmly believed that they were the ultimate pinnacle of creation. If there was a creator, surely he must have made man in his own image."

"So, when I appeared to a tribe of humans for the first time, I did so with my own image. They became so frightened, when they saw me, that they began running in blind terror. I flew after them trying to talk to them and calm them down. This only made things worse. In the end, they jumped off a cliff to escape and killed themselves. I was so appalled at what I had caused that I traveled back in time to just before the incident, and changed my appearance to a more human one."

"This changed history and the people did not die, but somehow, the trauma of that first encounter became part of the myth of humankind from then on. Try as I might, I have never been able to completely remove that image from the collective racial memory of humanity."

"Okay, now you really have my curiosity up. What do you look like? Let me see your true appearance. I promise not to go running and screaming over a cliff."

He was laughing again. "Yes, you would probably be one of the few humans that would see the irony and humor in it. So be it!"

His image wavered and blurred slightly for a moment. As it cleared, I gasped, and then began to laugh. Yes, I guess even God can make a mistake. He was about seven feet tall, with red skin and dark black eyes. He had wings that had a leathery look to them, two ivory white horns protruding from the top of his head, and a three foot long, barbed tail. How ironic indeed. Because of his one miscalculation, our God's true appearance had been linked with Satan ever since.

7.

<u>Words alone mean</u>
<u>nothing. Therefore,</u>
<u>speak with your</u>
<u>actions and your</u>
<u>words will be</u>
<u>believed.</u>
<u>The Book of Life</u>

I was still chuckling as I returned to my own time. I felt better, at that moment, about what had been happening to me, than I had since it had begun. I was looking forward to seeing Laura and filling her in on what had happened on my journey. I had missed her company and her unique sense of humor. As my thoughts centered on her, I suddenly had a feeling of pain and danger. I reached out to her mentally, but could not quite connect with her. I could feel her presence in our house, but she seemed to be unconscious.

I did not want to re-enter my body until I could determine what was going on, so I simply stepped through the wall into the living room and looked around. At first everything looked normal, except there was no light in the house at all. All the window shades were drawn and all the lights were out. This was unusual, since both Laura and I loved having the windows open to let in the fresh air and sunlight. Since we had no neighbors close around, we almost never closed the shades, even at night.

I glided on into the kitchen and saw a half empty pot of coffee on the coffee maker. The glowing red light on the unit showed that it was still on. It was dark here also and unnaturally quiet. Again I mentally reached out for Laura, and this time got a very weak response. She was alive! The quick impression I got from her was "Bedroom ... danger!" I was into our bedroom almost as fast as I could think it.

I was at ceiling height, looking down on our bed. Below me was Laura, with her hands and feet tied, and looking as if she were in a deep sleep. Next to her on the bed was my body. There were electrodes attached to my head, which ran to a portable EEG. Watching this device was a man about 30 to 35 years old, very muscular, wearing a dark blue suit. He also had a bedside tray set up with several syringes on it. He was obviously waiting for the EEG to show a change in brain activity, indicating that I had returned to my body. I was sure that the instant that happened, he fully intended to use one of those needles to sedate me.

Of course, as long I was still in my spirit form, he could do nothing to my body. On closer inspection, I could see a couple of broken syringes that testified to his inability to break the skin on my arm. I was not sure how he had managed to capture Laura. He must have caught her when she was sleeping, and injected her before she could leave her body.

I searched the rest of the bedroom for more intruders. When I was sure he was the only one, I picked up one of his own needles and injected him. I mentally reached into his throat and paralyzed his vocal chords, so he could not call for help, and then blocked the nerves going to his legs. He fell into a heap on the floor, tried to scream for a few minutes and then became unconscious. To make sure no one else could get into the bedroom until I was ready, I mentally rearranged the atoms of the wood in the bedroom door, so that it merged with the wood of the door frame. What used to be the door was now a seamless piece of solid oak. Not even a battering ram could get through now.

I quickly checked Laura to make sure she was ok. Outside of a bruise on her left cheek, she appeared to be unharmed. I would check her out from head to toe once the crisis was over, but for now I was convinced that she was in no immediate danger. I picked up one of the unused syringes from the bedside tray and mentally altered the chemical structure of the substance within. It was now a mild stimulant, instead of a sedative, and I injected Laura with it. She would regain consciousness in about ten minutes.

With my concern for Laura's safety temporarily satisfied, I turned my attention to the rest of the house. I spread my consciousness throughout every room, looking for anyone else that might be inside. I found two other men in one of the guest bedrooms. As I entered the room, one of the men was watching a screen that seemed to be some kind of motion detector, while the other was talking on a telephone. I entered the mind of the one on the phone and found that he was talking to another man, located in a van parked about half way up the road to our house. I swept through his mind to make sure there were no others and then put him quietly to sleep.

As he fell over on the bed, his partner jumped up from his chair, pulled out a rather nasty looking hand gun, and began wildly searching the room with his eyes. I materialized right in front of him about six feet away. He certainly had quick reactions, I'll give him that. He blinked once and then fired three shots point blank at my chest. I laughed and looked down. I had stopped the bullets about half an inch short of entering my body, where my heart should have been. They were just hovering in place, as if they were frozen in a block of ice.

"Nice grouping!" I said.

He swallowed, looked me in the eye, pissed his pants, and said, "Oh shit."

I smiled, said "Good night, sweet prince!" and rendered him

unconscious as well.

I secured the door to this room the same way I had in our bedroom, and changed the window glass into bullet proof plastic. These two would not be leaving until I was ready for them to. This left one more, the guy in the van. As I reached the vehicle, I simply opened the door, grabbed him by the back of his coat, lifted him off the ground, and flew him back to the house. I opened the door to the guest room, where his two friends were, put him to sleep, placed him on the floor, and secured the door again. Then I went down to the kitchen and grabbed a cup of black coffee, which I carried back up to our bedroom.

Laura was just starting to stir on the bed, as I came in. I kissed her gently and handed her the coffee. She took a couple of sips and then set the cup down on the table. She threw her arms around me and hugged me to her. She was sobbing quietly and kissing me all over my face and neck.

"I'm so glad to see you!" She said. "Are you ok?"

That was so typical of her. She had been through the wringer, but she wanted to know if I was ok.

"I smiled from ear to ear and said, "Yes, honey, I'm fine. Everything's under control now. What happened here? I go away for a few days and you decide to take in boarders?"

"Very funny!" She said. She motioned towards the man on the floor and said, "He came in while I was sleeping and hit me with an electric stun gun. Before I could recover, he had me sedated and tied up. I think there were others as well. Have you checked the rest of the house?"

"Yes, there were three others. They are all in one of the spare bedrooms and temporarily incapacitated. As soon as you are feeling a little better, we'll gather them all up and find out what's going on. Did they say anything to you or ask any questions?"

"No, they kept me pretty much unconscious most of the time. I got the feeling they were not willing to take any chances on my being able to defend myself or to somehow warn you."

"How long ago did this happen?"

She glanced at the alarm clock on the night stand and said, "It must be about nine hours ago. I heard a noise just before I got shocked and glanced up at the clock. It was about 3:15 AM then, and it's a little after noon now. I wonder, what's going on? These guys are certainly not burglars. They look and act more like CIA types than anything else."

"Yes," I said. "That is exactly what they seem like to me as well. They are too well organized and equipped to be anything else. If not CIA, they are certainly some form of secret governmental agency, but there is no need to guess. If you are ready, leave your body and grab this guy. I'll grab the other three and we'll take them outside down by the creek."

"What do you have in mind?" She asked.

I smiled and said, "We are going to get some answers, and teach them some respect for others at the same time."

We gathered them up and levitated them down to a small clearing in the trees next to the creek that ran through our property. Three of them were still unconscious, but the one that had soiled his underwear was coming around. Laura was looking at me with a strange half grin, as I set about the task of preparing our guests for the questioning. I looked at her and winked, as I mentally sent her the message to trust me and go along with whatever I said. As I finished the preparations and started bringing them all back to consciousness, she giggled and sent me the message, "Damn, honey! I'm glad you're on my side."

As each one of them opened their eyes, they all did the same thing. First they tried to move their legs, then they looked down to where their legs should be, and then they screamed. That was to be expected since in place of legs, they now had what appeared to be the trunk of a tree from about the waist down, rooted in the ground. I let them scream for about a minute and then changed the lips of three of them into a patch of tree bark. They could no longer scream. The pants pisser looked at me, rolled his eyes, and said, "Oh my God!"

I walked over and looked him in the eye and said, "Not exactly, but closer than you know!"

"Please!" he said, "Have mercy on us. Please change us back!!!"

"I might be so persuaded, providing I get some answers that I believe. You come onto our property uninvited, break into our home, abuse and then imprison my wife, attempt to shoot me, and you have the nerve to cry for mercy? Let me warn you that I can get the answers I want from you any number of ways, some more unpleasant for you than others. I could go straight into your mind and get the information I want, but I really do not like doing that if I don't have to. So, talk to me, and make it the truth the first time. Otherwise, I will complete your transformation, and you and your partners can become permanent dog urinals right here."

Well, needless to say, he talked, and he talked, and he talked. The poor man was so frightened that I started to feel bad about what I was putting him through, until I looked over at Laura and remembered what they had done to her. They were CIA, but were part of a "Black Ops" division that did not answer to the normal chain of command. Their unit had been formed about 30 years ago right after the President and the CIA had become aware of the fact that there were people around with, what seemed to them, magic powers. This was the story Laura had told me about right after we were married. This group had been searching for people like Laura and I ever since.

It seems that it had occurred to someone about ten years ago that people like us might be able to use the state lotteries to become wealthy. So they had been checking into all the big winners for years now, all over the country. When I won $52,000,000 and then soon after married a woman, who had also been a big winner a little over a year before, they became suspicious enough to want to pick us up and find out if it was just good luck on our part, or something else. They were to report back to their superiors within two days. If they did not, others would be sent to look for them, and us.

By the time he had finished his story, he was sobbing. He said they had been told that we could be dangerous and that we were to be knocked unconscious immediately. Then we were to be drugged and questioned. If we turned out to be what they were looking for, we were to be brought back to their headquarters unconscious. If we turned out to be just a couple of lucky people, they were to use drugs to wipe out all memory of what had happened.

I sat back on the grass and sighed. His story had the ring of truth to it and I believed him. The only questions left were had they talked to any of their people, after finding out that we were indeed what they were looking for, and what do I do with them? I could not afford to take their word about whether or not others knew about us. I pulled Laura aside and explained what we needed to do. She did not like it, but she agreed that we had no choice.

We each worked on two of them. One by one, we entered their minds and searched through all their memories, since they first arrived at our house. By the time we were done, we had satisfied ourselves that they had not had a chance to communicate any of their findings to anyone else. Finally, some good news! It meant that we had a chance to contain this mess and, perhaps, rectify the whole thing.

Laura hugged me to her and said, "So what do we do with them? I know you don't intend to leave them like that, but we can't just turn them loose. If we do, we will never be able to stop looking over our shoulders, and they will never give up as long as we live."

"No, I won't leave them like this, much as they might deserve it. I've just spent a lot of time with someone who is real big on compassion and forgiveness. It kind of rubs off on you after a while. I do have an idea, though. Let's get them back to the house and I'll explain what I'm going to do."

I changed them all back into their normal forms and knocked them out again. We took them back to the house and I gathered up all their equipment into one room. First, I concocted a plausible scenario for the benefit of their superiors. It went something like this. They had arrived and found us both asleep in bed. They stunned us both, then drugged us. They questioned us and found that we were just two ordinary people, who happened to be lucky enough to hit the lottery. We met in a bar, dated for a while, fell in love, and got married. Ho hum, white bread, la de da, normal. The end!

Then I took their video camera and caused the images of my fairy tale to be imprinted on the video tape. Finally, I sat all four of our guests up on the couch, set their minds on record, so to speak, and made them watch the video tape I had created. They would now believe what was on the video tape was exactly what had happened. Each one of them would fill in any details of what they were doing, while this was happening, and would never be able to tell that this was a false memory. So, they would all tell the same story to their superiors, and it would be corroborated by the video tape. We were clear! Their last memory of us would be that they had erased our memory of their visit and had left us asleep in bed.

So, we watched them load all their equipment into the van

and drive away. I locked everything up and Laura and I went back upstairs to the bedroom. We popped back into our bodies and lay for a few minutes in a silent embrace, there on the bed. Finally, I kissed her gently and said, "God, I missed you!"

She snuggled up closer to me and said, "Oh yeah? Prove it!"

So, I did.

8.

<u>Love may lie</u>
<u>dormant for a</u>
<u>while, but evil</u>
<u>never sleeps.</u>
<u>The Book of Life</u>

"Damn! Where's that coffee I asked for? How am I ever supposed to find these freaks, when the people they give me to work with can't even get me a cup of coffee, when I ask for it?"

Muttering to himself, Richard Wilkinson stepped to the door of his office, stuck his head out, and yelled at his assistant, "You! Shit head! Where's my coffee? And where the fuck are those assholes I sent to Colorado? They were supposed to have been here half an hour ago. There's gonna be hell to pay, if they aren't standing in front of my desk in the next ten minutes. Find 'em! Now!! And for Christ's sake, somebody get me some fucking coffee!!!"

He slammed the door and walked to the window. It was just about 8:00 AM and the sun was making a valiant effort to penetrate the cloud layer. The traffic on the streets below was still snarled from rush hour and it was starting to sprinkle rain. Wilkinson had not slept for almost three days. He was the head of the covert operations group, whose responsibility was to locate, capture, and study people with "special" abilities. He answered only to the President and was given a great deal of latitude. He enjoyed the power that this position granted him and he devoted himself to it completely.

He hated sleeping. He wanted to know what was going on and to be in control 24 hours a day. When he did sleep, it was seldom more than three hours. He took pills to help stay awake, and he drank coffee constantly. This did nothing to improve his mood of course. He was a hard man under the best of circumstances, but when he decided to stay awake for days at a time, the pills made him dangerous to be around. Even the hardened CIA types that worked for him were quick to leave the area, when he showed any signs of an eruption.

Of course, the main reason he slept so little was because he feared what might happen to him, while he was unconscious. His mind drifted back to that day about 30 years ago, which had changed the course of his life forever. He had been called into a meeting with the President himself, along with the heads of the Pentagon and the Director of the CIA. He had done work for the President of a covert and highly sensitive nature, but had never before been summoned into his presence. He had always received his assignments through others. This change made him nervous!

Then the President had briefed them. He told them about a man, who had simply appeared out of thin air right in front of him and the Director of the CIA, had levitated objects, and performed other miracles. It had taken some time to convince everyone that the President had not had a breakdown of some kind, but eventually they were convinced. Everyone, that is, except Wilkinson.

He was not sure why the President felt the need to concoct this ridiculous story, but it did not matter. He would do what was required of him regardless. After all, they had used that magic phrase which made him tingle with excitement, "National Security!" If the President wanted to invent demi-gods as a reason for this action, so be it. One did not succeed in his line of work by questioning orders. One thing was certain. The President was one hell of an actor. He really looked and sounded as if he were frightened of this person.

The other's job was to party with this individual, when he returned to the White House that evening. They were to flatter him and keep filling his glass with champagne. Of course, the champagne would be drugged. It was a special drug that acted quickly and for which everyone at the party, except the guest of honor, would have already taken the antidote. They would be unaffected, but the honoree would pass out rather quickly. That was when his part would start.

He was to take charge of the prisoner, and have him moved to a Company owned and run psychiatric hospital. There they had a ward in the sub-basement, where he would be interrogated. This was one of his areas of specialization. Some drugs would be used, but they would be mostly to keep the prisoner sedated and a little more compliant. His techniques for the giving of pain were many and varied, and he was very good at it. Everyone had a breaking point, and he eventually found it. His blending of physical and mental torture had never failed to produce results.

The man had resisted longer than Wilkinson would have believed he was capable of. When he first regained consciousness, he simply looked puzzled. He could not understand what had happened to him and why he was strapped down to what appeared to be an operating table. He seemed to be convinced that there was some kind of mistake that had been made, and if he explained who he was, they would realize their error and let him go.

"Hey, you guys are making a big mistake. I am working with the President! The President of the United States!! When he finds out what you're doing, there will be hell to pay!!! Lemme GO, assholes!!!"

Wilkinson had merely smiled and replied, "Who do you think

sent you here? Your life, as you know it, has definitely ended. Why not save yourself some major discomfort and just tell us what we want to know?"

"I ain't tellin' you shit, till you let me loose. What the hell do you want from me anyway?"

With a look like a student examining a curious new specimen of fungus under a microscope, Wilkinson replied, "Everything! I want it all. How did you do that disappearing trick? How did you levitate objects? Where did you learn to do this? How many others do you know who can do the same things? What are their names? Where do they live? Who do you work for? Are you now or have you ever been a member of the Communist Party? How long will it take you to teach us how to do these things? All these things, and many more, you will tell me. How much mind and body you still have available to you at the end of the process is up to you. So, what's it to be?"

Wilkinson laughed to himself as he remembered, the dick head had spit in his face. All balls and no brains! He had calmly wiped it from his face and picked up a dentist's drill. As he turned it on and approached the man's face, the guy had finally realized he was in deep shit. When he saw the unnatural light in Wilkinson's eyes, almost like lust, he had begun to beg. Wilkinson shivered, as he fondly remembered the man's terror.

"Well, I guess I can't blame you for not understanding. After all, we don't know each other very well yet, do we? Let me share one of my hobbies with you. I always wanted to be a dentist, when I was a kid. I never actually went to school for it, but I still love to get in some practice, when I can. Sorry that I have no Novocain to give you, but we won't let that stop us will we? If the pain gets too bad, go ahead and scream; I promise I won't be annoyed by it. After that, we'll talk again. Maybe, by that time, we will know each other better and you will be willing to behave in a friendlier manner."

A tentative knock at the door brought him back to the present. "What?" he screamed. The door opened and there was the new guy, Turner, with a cup of coffee in his hand. He walked closer and handed the cup to Wilkinson.

"Here's your coffee, sir. The four agents you inquired about, are just a few blocks away now. They should be here within the next 10 minutes. Is there anything else I can do for you, sir?"

"Yes. You can quit licking my boots and get out!"

The man fairly flew out the door. Wilkinson gulped at the coffee and walked back to the window, chuckling. He did so enjoy his job. He held the coffee cup in both hands and sipped at it now, slowly, as his thoughts drifted back to that day once again. The steam rising from the cup reminded him of the smoke that had billowed from the man's mouth, as the drill penetrated layer after layer of tooth enamel. Each time it broke through to the nerve, the man had screamed, as though his entire life force was emanating from his throat. He finally had to stop, because the idiot's tongue had hit the drill so many times, Wilkinson was afraid that he might not be able to form intelligible words any longer, and that just would not do. So he poured a generous amount of scotch into the fool's mouth, listened to him scream again, then said, "Rest now for a while, and we'll talk again."

He ordered another sedative injection for the prisoner and then left him there to think about things for a while. The guards in the room looked ill and would not meet his eyes, when he looked at them. Good! If they feared him, they would obey him without question. He had decided long ago that respect and obedience were products of fear. He gave orders to call his office, if the prisoner started talking while he was gone, and then left the room.

Once again, a knock at the door brought him back to the here and now. It damn sure better be those four agents, or whoever was on the other side of the door would be sorry for interrupting his thought processes. He opened the door to find the overdue agents standing so straight that they appeared to be at attention.

"Well, well, well; nice of you to join me, ladies. Please, come in, come in. Won't you join me for tea?"

They looked at each other as if they were seeking some kind of verification that each had heard what the other had heard. Then, almost as one, they turned back to him and said, "Yes, sir!" and walked through the door uneasily.

He held the door open for them, as they marched in. He turned to see the entire office looking at him, as if he had just sprouted horns. He looked at Turner and said, "Well, you heard the gentlemen, Turner. Get them some tea, and bring more coffee for me. Oh, and Turner, if you hear screaming, just knock once and leave the tray outside the door, won't you? There's a good lad!"

He closed the door gently behind him and turned to stare at the four men standing quietly in front of his desk. He walked slowly to his chair, sat down, straightened the creases in his trouser legs, adjusted his vest, and picked up the report lying on his desk. He read through it for effect only. He had already read it several times. Finally, he laid it back down in the center of the desk, and arranged it in a neat pile. He steepled his fingers and said, "Report!"

"Sir!" began the one called Adamson. "There is nothing to report. We checked them out, as ordered. They are clean! Just a couple of very lucky people."

"Is that the video tape of your questioning of the subjects?"

"Yes, sir!" said Adamson, as he handed him the tape. "I believe you will find everything in order, sir."

Wilkinson looked up at the man standing before him and noticed the small beads of perspiration on his forehead and upper lip. The man did not seem to want to make eye contact with him and seemed ill at ease. While Wilkinson was very aware of his effect on the men that worked for him, something just did not feel right here. He surveyed the other three agents in the room and they too seemed to avoid looking directly at him.

"All in order, eh? Did they give you any trouble?"

They all looked at each other and then back at him, and said, "No, sir."

"Jamisson! Did you erase all memories of your visit?"

Looking like a boot camp recruit standing at attention, Jamisson replied, "Yes, sir! They will remember nothing."

Wilkinson was starting to get angry! There was something not right here. They were holding something back, and it was really starting to piss him off.

"Did one of you or all of you bone the bitch?"

They actually looked surprised at that one. Adamson finally looked directly at him and said, "No, sir! We would never do anything to endanger a mission, sir; you know that."

Then rising slowly to his feet, he rounded the desk and stood toe to toe with Adamson. He could feel the adrenaline starting to pump into his muscles. The pupils of his eyes were beginning to dilate and his breathing was speeding up, to supply his body with the oxygen it needed for the burst of violence that now seemed imminent. Speaking in a very tight, controlled voice that was hardly above a whisper he said, "Then what? What are you dick heads holding back?"

Adamson started to look back at the others, and that was just the wrong move. Wilkinson flexed his wrist a certain way, and the stiletto that he kept hidden in his sleeve, dropped into his hand in an instant. He moved the knife to Adamson's throat in a fluid motion. He applied just enough pressure to puncture the skin slightly and small drops of blood started to form and roll down the man's throat, and onto his white shirt collar.

"Don't look at them! I asked you a question. Answer me now, while you still can!"

He could hear the intake of breath from the other three men in the room. He glanced quickly at them, to see if they seemed inclined to move toward him. They did not! His lips pulled back from his teeth in what seemed to be more snarl than smile. He almost wished they would try. Trying desperately to speak, without causing any further damage to his throat, Adamson said, "Well, sir. This is not exactly how we planned to broach the subject, but, uh well, this was our last mission, sir. We would like to tender our resignations."

This took Wilkinson so much by surprise that he let go of Adamson and took three steps back, and went into a knife fighter's crouch, as if he had been physically attacked. Adamson lost no time in moving as far away from Wilkinson as the walls of the office would allow. He rubbed gingerly at the spot on his neck that was still oozing blood. His three partners quickly joined him.

"Resign? You resign? And your reason for resigning is...?"

The four men stared at him in silence for a moment. They looked as if they were trying to decide how to phrase their answers so as not to incite him to further displays of violence. True, there were four of them, but they had seen him in action many times. He was not a person you wanted to irritate, if it could be avoided. Jamisson finally answered for them all.

"Sir, this has been a difficult decision for us all. It is not something we do lightly, and our reasons for it are hard to put into words."

There was a knock at the door and Wilkinson said, "Come!" without even turning around. Turner walked in carrying the tea and coffee. He served them quietly and glanced nervously at the blood on Adamson's collar, but said nothing. He gave Wilkinson his coffee and quickly left the room. Wilkinson replaced the stiletto in his sleeve sheath and walked back to his desk, straightened his tie, and sat down in his chair. He motioned for the agents to sit, which they did, still watching him carefully.

Sipping at his coffee gave Wilkinson a chance to slow his body back down to normal and try to figure out exactly what was going on. They still had not completely answered his question. He decided to go at it from a slightly different direction.

"Well, I guess you aren't the first ones to want out, and probably won't be the last. I will be sorry to lose you, but shit happens! So tell me, what do you plan to do with the rest of your lives? There's not much call for your talents in the civilian world. How do you plan to make a living?"

This seemed to make them uncomfortable all over again. They looked at each other, then at him, then at the floor. Finally,

Jamisson spoke again.

"Well sir, there are a lot of problems out there and not many people really trying to make a difference. Our planet is dying and if we don't start trying to make things better, we will all pay the price."

Wilkinson stared at them, open mouthed. He looked as if he were not quite sure he had understood what they were saying. He tilted his head to one side, as if trying to see if it would make more sense from another angle and said, "Okay, so you're concerned about pollution. What do you intend to do about it?"

Another round of looking at each other and then they kind of shrugged, and Roberts spoke for the first time.

"Uh, well ... I ... that is we ... well we are kinda considering the field of," he glanced around at his compatriots one more time, took a deep breath and said, "Forestry."

Wilkinson looked as if he had been shot.

"Forestry? As in taking care of trees? As in Forest Rangers?"

They looked as if they wished for nothing so much at that moment as to be invisible, but they all nodded their heads, and said, "Yes, sir."

Something was way off kilter here. These four men had worked for him for several years now. He knew their profiles well, and nowhere was there ever any mention of a desire to get back to nature. Either they were playing some kind of game with him, which would have meant a death wish that was also not in their bios, or else something drastic had happened to them, while they had been on assignment. This being a little more likely a scenario, he decided not to kill them, at least, not right this moment.

"So, tell me, gentlemen, why forest rangers? Why not open a bar, or a liquor store, or a massage parlor? Reilly, you've never been interested in the great outdoors before. I remember you bitching like hell that time I sent you to the Amazon. I seem to recall you saying to someone, quote, "If man had been meant to live in the jungle, then why did God invent cities?" unquote. What has changed?"

"We asked these same questions of each other, sir. None of us has ever been particularly interested in nature, per se. We don't really understand it either, except that while we were surrounded by all those trees in Colorado, we suddenly realized that trees are important. They produce most of the oxygen for our planet. All we know is that someone has to protect them, sir! I guess we figure it might as well be us as anyone else."

All during Reilly's little speech Wilkinson had been

watching Adamson, Roberts, and Jamisson. As Reilly's fervor had increased, their eyes had grown wider, their nostrils flared, and their breathing had quickened. They obviously agreed with his sentiments completely. He had seen fanaticism many times before. He had used it to further his goals on occasion. The same insanity, which lit up the eyes of the Irish Catholics talking about the sins of the Protestants in a pub in Belfast, was also present in these four men. Something had altered them. They had not been gone long enough for normal brainwashing techniques to have been employed. No, this was too much, too fast. Something smelled here.

He stood up and pressed a button on his intercom. He looked at the four idiots standing there, breathing hard and broadcasting righteousness, and he knew what he had to do. They had obviously been successful in their search for the freaks. They had been altered in a way that no normal human could accomplish. The door opened and he turned to them and said, "I want the four of you to go for debriefing. When that has been completed, you can go where ever you want and hug the trees till you fucking croak for all I care. Turner, I want separate depositions, in separate rooms. I want a printout of each one on my desk by 7:00 AM tomorrow. Dismissed!"

As they all filed out of his office, he picked up his coffee cup and went back to the window. He was deep in his planning mode now. As soon as he was satisfied that he had gotten every last detail he could from them, Adamson, Roberts, Jamisson, and Reilly must be eliminated. They carried too much knowledge, about too many sensitive subjects, to be allowed to run around loose. When a man suddenly develops morals in this business, he becomes dangerous to the Company. It was a shame, really. Those four men had served him well on many missions, though he would never have admitted it to anyone.

What had those freaks done to them? He would find a way to exact some justice from them for this. The problem was, they were so close to being all powerful that there was almost no way to get your hands on them, but there were some weaknesses. Certain drugs, including alcohol, could render them temporarily powerless. They also still had human emotions. That was a major weakness, and he fully intended to take advantage of it.

His mind went back to the interrogation of the first one. The fool had actually told the President about the effects of drugs and alcohol on their abilities. So, he had ordered the prisoner to be constantly sedated. Wilkinson had not let him have more than two hours of rest, after the first round of questioning. He had the man stripped and secured to the operating table again. When he walked in and put himself back into the prisoner's line of vision, the man had almost fainted at the sight of him. Good, the initial meeting had produced the desired effect, total fear. He put on his friendliest face and leaned down over the man.

"So, my friend, ready to talk some more? I do hope so, for your sake. All I require is total cooperation, and I will see to it that you get all the medical attention you need, to stop the pain. You are very valuable to us, you know. Once you are part of the team, we will take excellent care of you. You have my word on that! Now, how did you learn to do all these tricks, hmm?"

The man began to cry and shake his head no. Wilkinson walked over to a small table with several surgical instruments laid out on it, and picked up a scalpel. As he returned to the operating table, the prisoner began to beg. Wilkinson tested the scalpel by shaving a small amount of hair from the prisoner's chest with it.

"Ok, let's try this one more time."

He reached down and took hold of the man's scrotum. Handling the scalpel with great finesse, he sliced off a layer of skin only a few centimeters thick, from the right testicle. He held it up to let the man see what he had done, then laid it on his chest.

"I am quite good with a scalpel. I can peel your balls like peeling an onion, one layer at a time. If that does not convince you to cooperate, I will begin slicing the head of your penis, like I would a dill pickle to go on a hamburger. Oh, don't worry. I'll leave you enough to piss with, but that will be about the extent of it."

He reached over and picked up an alcohol swab and swiped it across the cut he had just made. The man screamed and started thrashing against his bonds, as though he were trying to come right out of his skin.

"Come now, there is no need for all of this. In the end, you will tell me what I want to know. You know that as well as I do. Why not save yourself all this needless pain? No one could blame you. Most people would not have resisted as long as you have. There can be only one outcome, so tell me. How many others like you are there?"

The man sobbed, as if his whole reason for living had been taken away from him. Wilkinson looked into his eyes and knew he had won. The man was broken. He would tell him anything he wanted to know now.

"I'm not sure, exactly, somewhere around eight or nine hundred. Please, give me something for the pain, please."

Wilkinson motioned for the guard and sent him for the doctor. In the meantime, he gave the man an injection of morphine. The effect was almost immediate.

"There, that's better isn't it? You see? I can be reasonable when I get what I want. I have sent for the doctor to treat your wounds. Just a couple more questions before he gets here, then we'll get you fixed up and let you rest up for a while. You said there are others like you. How are you trained to develop these powers?"

"We are not trained. The powers come on their own, when you reach a certain stage in your personal evolution. The others are only there to help you learn what is happening to you. It always starts with the dreams. The change always starts in your dreams."

"Where is your headquarters located?"

The man looked puzzled. "What do you mean, headquarters?"

"Headquarters, main office, control center. You know what I mean. Where there is an organization, there is always a headquarters. Where is it?"

"That is not an easy question to answer. I guess you would say it is in another dimension. It is not a physical place, exactly. You can only get there when you are out of body."

"Out of body? Never mind, we'll get back to that later. The doctor is here. One last thing, names. I want the names of your compatriots, so we can start rounding them up."

The man started crying again. "Please, don't ask me that. These people are like family to me. They have taken care of me and helped me keep my sanity through all of this. Please, don't make me do this."

Wilkinson was about to remind him that he could easily send the doctor away and begin the questioning with the scalpel again, when the straps securing the man to the operating table had suddenly snapped. He floated up into the air and there were what appeared to be three men floating next to him. One gestured toward the ceiling and a hole appeared, all the way up through the roof. No explosion, no falling debris; just an opening. He heard the prisoner say, "Thank God!" as he and two of the men floated up through the hole, and out of sight. The third man was hovering about six inches above the floor, three feet in front of him, motionless, and staring at him.

Wilkinson hesitated, only a fraction of a second, and then sprang at the man, scalpel at the ready. He sliced at the carotid artery and, at the same time, aimed a kick at the groin. At the very least the man should have been immediately incapacitated, and quite possibly would have bled to death rather quickly. The only problem was, both the scalpel and the kick passed right through the man, as if there was nothing there but air. Wilkinson hit the ground, rolled a short distance, and came up in a fighting crouch, scalpel at the ready. The man was still hovering in the same spot. He was not smiling.

"You, sir are quite a piece of work, aren't you?"

Wilkinson grinned and said, "You have no idea. What now? I suppose you intend to kill me."

Now the man did smile!

"No, no. Much too easy, and you learn nothing that way. I have a better idea."

The man gestured toward him and simply said, "Sleep!"

When he had awoken, everyone was gone and there was no longer a hole in the ceiling. His first reaction upon awaking was to scream, over and over again. Minute by minute he was reliving what he had done to the prisoner, but not his memories. It was as if he had become the prisoner. He could see his own face leering down at him holding up a piece of his own testicle. Every thought, every pain the man had experienced were now being replayed in his own mind, as real as if it had actually happened to him.

Coming back to the present again, his mind focused once more on the task at hand. Yes, he remembered. He could never forget what they had done to him. He had been afraid to sleep ever since. That was when he had dedicated the rest of his life to the task of finding and totally eradicating these freaks. That had been thirty years ago. Now, for the first time since then, he had a real lead on a couple of them.

9.

<u>All the universe</u>
<u>strives for</u>
<u>balance. Therefore,</u>
<u>seek after</u>
<u>goodness, but be</u>
<u>not blind to evil.</u>
The Book of Life

We did our best to put what had happened behind us and get on with our lives. Laura was a little shaken up, but I was the one most affected by it. I could not help but wonder, what would have happened had I been home in bed with her that night, instead of on my time trip. The best case scenario was that we would have been nothing better than lab rats for some time to come. Worst case? I still do not want to think about it!

The thing that bothered me most was that the longer I thought about what had happened, the angrier I became. Thank God Laura's bruises faded quickly. Every time I saw them I got mad all over again. I can deal with the idea that someone might want to cause me harm, but I cannot understand why anyone would want to hurt her. She is the most gentle and loving person, I have ever met and harbors no ill will toward anyone. She was actually worried about what we had done to her attackers and how it might affect them. The very thought that anyone would try to hurt such a loving soul, made me tremble with rage. I resolved that even God could not save them from me, if they ever tried such a thing again!

Of course, Laura was aware that something was bothering me. She knew me so well that I could hide nothing from her, even if I wished to do so. She finally convinced me that we needed a vacation. Actually, it didn't take much convincing. I knew that I would soon be starting Godhood School and that I would have little free time after that. So, I was more than willing to spend some time luxuriating in her company and rediscovering just how lucky we were to have each other.

Laura started packing our suitcases, while I called the airlines for tickets and made reservations for us in a small, but very expensive resort in Tahiti. I told her to pack light. We would buy whatever we needed when we got there. I just wanted to get going and get away from the recent memories for a while. Being rich does indeed have its advantages. I seldom even noticed the cost of things any more.

With all the arrangements made, I wandered into the bedroom to help Laura pack. She was humming softly, as she moved quickly around the room. I stood leaning against the door jamb, with my arms folded across my chest, and just watched her for a few minutes. There was nothing fragile about Laura, nor did she appear to be a "Little girl lost". Yet, she aroused in me the most intense protective urges, I had ever experienced. In fact, she was eminently capable of protecting herself, but that did not change the way I felt standing there watching her.

She finally noticed me standing there and skipped over to me, threw her arms around me, and kissed me. She smiled and said, "I can't wait to get there! I'm going to spend a whole day doing nothing, but lying in the sun. Your job will be to keep me well oiled, so I don't burn."

I laughed and said, "Crap! I go all the way to Tahiti, and all I get to do is rub oil all over my semi-nude wife's beautiful body, all day long. The sacrifices I make, just to keep you happy, are without end!"

She started laughing and tickling me, and we ended up landing on the bed. Being the more expert tickler, I landed on top. She squirmed underneath me and said, "Okay, that's enough. Let me up! I need to finish packing."

I pinned her to the bed and said, "Ooooh, move like that again!"

I started kissing her face and slowly started working my way down. I kept her pinned down with one hand and started removing clothing with the other. She struggled briefly, but her heart was not in it.

"You cheat!" she said. "You know I'm not strong enough to make you stop."

She sighed and pulled me even closer, giving me that look that she knew melted my heart and turned my blood to liquid fire. My pulse began to race and my heart was filled with the nearness of her. I reached out with my mind and partially linked with her. Her pupils dilated, her breath came faster, and she shivered from head to toe. We were sharing bodily sensations. What I felt, she felt, and vice versa. The physical sensations were double what most people ever feel, but that was only the beginning. To be able to share the love, to be able to feed back and forth from one to the other, to truly share one's self completely with another elevates love making to a mystical experience beyond description.

Forty-five minutes later, we were finally able to disengage from each other. As she started to rise from the bed, she leaned over and looked straight into my eyes. Her eyes were wide open and the pupils were dilated, with the tiniest hint of tears beginning to form. Before I could ask her what was wrong, she kissed me hard and said, "I want you to know how much I love you! You do know that I would not want to live without you, don't you? I want you to hear from my own lips how lucky I feel to even know you, much less share your life. Never, ever forget, for even a moment, how much you mean to me."

I was so taken aback at this declaration that I simply stared at her for a moment in disbelief. Then I reached out and touched her cheek, so softly, and the tears did come to my eyes.

"Oh my love, what have I ever done to deserve such a prize? Live without me??? No power anywhere could make that happen. I would literally move heaven and earth to be at your side. What would ever posses you to make such a statement?"

"I'm not sure, but I have this weird feeling that someone or something may try to separate us in the near future."

I looked at her, and worried. She was not prone to such feelings without reason. I could only shrug and reply, "God help anyone who tries!"

She rose from the bed, wiping her eyes, and said, "This is nuts! I'm still just nervous over what happened. Come on, get up. We still have a lot of packing to do. We're on vacation, remember? Unless you plan to take up nudism, we'd better get dressed and get moving, so move it big boy!"

Unbelievable! That fast she was back up, skipping around the room, and humming again. I chuckled to myself and began getting dressed, but I could not resist one last pinch of her derriere, as she whizzed by me. She turned and looked at me, and then it was her turn to giggle.

"You may have some problems getting your pants on in that condition sir."

"It's all your fault, Madame. I do believe that you will need to get dressed, before I decide to cancel the reservations, and simply lock us in here for the next couple of weeks."

The next hour was a blur of activity. Somehow we managed to get packed and get to the airport in time to make the last flight to Tahiti. As we settled into our seats, we were finally able to relax again. We napped in each other's arms most of the way and were just starting to be fully awake again, when we landed. As we stepped off the plane, we were immediately struck by the beauty of the sunset. As we headed for our hotel, little did we dream what was happening back at our home.

We had been invaded! Men in black coveralls were swarming all over the house. They were installing listening devices throughout every room. The phones were now tapped. There were even state of the art miniature video cameras hidden in the heating ducts and behind walls that could see through a hole barely larger than one made by a paneling nail. There were canisters of an anesthetic gas also hidden with switches that would allow them to be activated by remote control. The gas was colorless and odorless, and would render an adult human unconscious within 10 seconds of the first inhalation.

Richard Wilkinson walked calmly amidst the flurry of activity around him. He had decided to oversee this job personally. He watched especially carefully the installation of the plastic explosives being placed in the basement of the house. He was not the least afraid of a premature explosion. His only concerns were that the explosives be disguised well enough not to draw attention to them, and that there was enough to level the structure and kill every living thing within it, right down to the cockroaches and houseplants.

Of course, there was still the possibility that he was over reacting. He had no actual evidence that these two people were anything other than normal. In fact, he had a lot of evidence that this was exactly the case. Never the less, he did not believe the evidence at hand. The sudden change of his former and now deceased operatives, from cold blooded assassins to forest ranger wannabe's, had convinced him that something was not kosher here. So he had ordered this mission to help him gather further information. After all, what good was it having this huge budget, and all this high tech equipment, if you never used it?

He had placed a trace on all their credit card transactions, so he had been aware of their impending trip from the moment the reservations had been made. This had presented him with the perfect opportunity to get in here and get everything set up, with no fear of being discovered in the process. He had two agents on the same flight with them, to keep an eye on them until they returned, but he threatened them with summary execution, if they were discovered. He could not afford to tip his hand before he was ready. If these people were what he suspected they might be, they were dangerous beyond belief.

There would be video cameras hidden in some of the trees surrounding the home as well. They had set up a command post and surveillance station in a small cabin, just about a mile away. Nothing and no one would be able to come or go inside or outside this house, without his knowing about it.

He had seen absolutely nothing here that would contribute to his suspicions about this couple. He thought back to his reaction when he had first walked into the house. The hairs on the back of his neck had stood up. He had that feeling that he remembered his mother describing, when he was a child, as if someone had just walked over your grave.

He had an instant of pure panic and wished nothing more

than to simply turn and run back to his office, and forget the whole thing. He had walked back outside for a moment and stood up against a tree, wiping the sweat from his forehead with a handkerchief. Seeing the men passing by him, glancing nervously in his direction out of the corner of their eyes, reassured him. After all, he also could be very dangerous. He had straightened his tie and walked back in to oversee the work. No spooky feelings would keep him from doing his job.

"Come on you dick heads, move your asses! Let's wrap this up and get out of here before they decide to come back. There had better not be one speck of dust out of place, when you finish either."

Seeing their instant doubling of effort as a result of his "Encouragement" made him smile. God, he loved his job! He recalled a line from an old comedy movie, that he had seen long ago, "It's good to be the king!"

Meanwhile, Laura had been true to her word. She had spent almost the entire first day of our vacation lying in the sun. Keeping my word to her, I kept her well covered with sun block and enjoyed every minute of it. The weather was perfect, not a cloud in the sky, with a high temperature of about 80°. The sunset was spectacular, with colors ranging from orange to dark red. We ate a catered supper on the beach that evening, with the sounds of the surf providing the perfect back drop to our conversation. The full moon provided enough light to see by with no problem. It was wonderful!

We had scheduled some scuba diving lessons for the next morning and were looking forward to it. The afternoon would be a shopping expedition into town, with the aid of a couple of scooters we had rented. A moonlight stroll on the beach was on tap for the evening. It was a great trip so far, so why was I still so tense? There was absolutely nothing wrong that I could put my finger on, but I had a mounting feeling that we were in danger somehow.

I made a real effort to try to keep this feeling from affecting our trip. Laura had been through enough without upsetting her with a hunch. She needed this trip to relieve some of the stress from her ordeal, and I needed it just to be close to her. So, I tried my best to get into the spirit of it, but I kept a close eye on what was going on around us anyway.

Wilkinson took one last look around the house, before he left. Everything was in order. The last of the workers had packed up his gear and left. The first watch of the surveillance teams had taken their place in the cabin and all the equipment had tested out perfectly. They were ready to go as soon as the subjects returned from their trip. He pulled out his handkerchief and wiped his fingerprints from the door knob, as he walked out, and locked the door behind him. He smiled at the reflex action. Old habits die hard. As he got into his car and drove away, he could not help but laugh to himself. He knew he was right about these two, and now he would prove it.

The day's adventures had worn Laura out. She was asleep with her head on my chest. Meanwhile, I had become more certain with every passing hour that something was not right. I had decided that if I was to have any peace on this vacation, I would have to make a little trip first. So, I slipped out of my body and headed home. I hovered over the outside of the house and checked everything out. There were small animals here and there, and an occasional deer, but no human presence anywhere on our property. Satisfied with this cursory check, I went inside and floated from room to room. No one there, nothing out of place, everything as it should be.

Ok, I'm paranoid, so sue me! I left our Colorado house and headed for the one outside Phoenix. I went through the same procedure again. Nothing, nada, zip! I could not shake this feeling that something was wrong, but I sure could not find anything either. I floated up to my old position above the city lights of Phoenix and thought about it for a while. What had I missed? Was I just being jumpy, because of what had happened to us recently?

"I thought I might find you here."

I smiled as I turned. It did not startle me as it had the last time this had happened, because I now recognized the voice.

"Hi honey, what are you doing here?"

"Looking for you! I woke up looking for a little midnight romance, and you were more than a little unresponsive. It didn't take me long to figure out why, so here I am."

She floated over and wrapped her arms around me. I pulled her close and kissed her gently.

"You're still worried, aren't you? I'll bet you've been to both houses tonight too. Did you find anything?"

I sighed and said, "Yes, I have been to both houses, and no, I did not find anything out of the ordinary."

"Then you've done all you can for now. So, let's go back to our room and you can scratch my itch. I know you feel something is wrong. I feel it too, but I don't want it to spoil what may be our last trip together for some time. I'll tell you what. When we get back home, you have to take a trip to Godhood School anyway. Why don't you go and have a chat with the Boss. If there is anyone who can help, I would think it would be Him."

"That's a great idea! Ok, I promise, no more night-time

wanderings for the rest of the trip."

As we floated off back toward the island and our hotel, I grabbed her and began swirling her round and round, as I created the sound of the Sleeping Beauty Waltz. We laughed and danced all the way back, as the words filled the night air around us.

"I know you. I walked with you once upon a dream ..."

10.

To partake of the
calm at the eye of
the storm, we must
endure the violence
of its departure
as well as its
arrival.
The Book of Life

So, I kept my word to Laura. I devoted all my energies, for the rest of the vacation, to being with her and enjoying our vacation. It was one of the best times I can remember, and I can remember a lot of time now. The weather was so beautiful that I could almost swear it had been special ordered for us. It was about 80° for a high each day, with little or no clouds, and it got down to about 65° at night. The sunsets were nothing short of spectacular. We did some sightseeing, shopping, dining, dancing, diving, bird watching, and an awful lot of laughing. We were like kids lost in paradise. Every day was a new adventure filled with promise and fulfillment.

We woke up on the day we were to return home at almost the same time. I opened my eyes to find Laura propped up on one elbow, watching me and smiling. I returned the smile, kissed her and said, "Good morning! Been awake long?"

"Nah! Just a few minutes. I have been trying to psych myself up for the trip home. It has been a great vacation, hasn't it?"

"Yes, it has been wonderful! We could always stay longer, if you wanted to."

She took a deep breath and sighed.

"Don't tempt me mister! No, it has been a time to remember, but it's time to leave. You have important matters that need attending to, and I am beginning to miss our home. It will begin to get cooler soon and it will be time to close up the house and move back to Arizona for the winter. We have a lot to do before that happens."

"Ok. You're right, as always, but there is no immediate rush. Let us savor these last few moments of peace together."

I pulled her closer and wrapped her in my arms. I could feel the warmth of her body against my chest. I buried my face in her hair and took in deep lungs full of the sweet smell that I have come to associate with her. I laid my hand on her chest and could feel the beating of her heart. Our eyes locked together for a moment and then her lips were gently pressed to mine. I could feel the warm rays of the sun shining through the window, like a golden caress against my skin. The breeze from the open window was cool and light. The combination was delicious in the extreme.

We lay there holding each other and making small, husband and wife talk for another hour. When we could postpone it no longer, we arose from the bed and started preparing for the trip home. Laura, being who she is, having finally decided it was time to go home had thrown herself into it completely, and was humming again. Every time I looked at her that day, I remember smiling from ear to ear, and reminding myself what a lucky S.O.B. I really am! When she would catch me smiling at her, she would just wink at me and keep on humming, and so it went.

We finally got everything packed up and ready to go. This was no easy task, because we had bought a lot, while we were there. We checked out of the hotel and gave our thanks and some outrageous tips to the staff, for a wonderful vacation. They smiled and bowed a lot, and put us into a taxi bound for the airport. When we arrived and were going through the check in procedures, I got the distinct feeling that we were being watched. I let Laura handle everything and began checking out the people around us. Even for someone with my abilities, a crowded airport is not an easy place to locate one person, who may or may not be watching you.

I finally felt as if I had narrowed it down to an area over by the telephone booths. I started searching the faces of the people on the phones, one by one, and gently touching their thoughts. I was looking for any hint of attention directed towards either Laura or I. There! The older man in the gray business suit. He was very intent on Laura. I moved into his thoughts a little deeper, and then started to chuckle.

Oh yeah, he was watching her all right. In fact, his eyes were glued to her posterior. He was on the phone to his wife, but his thoughts were all for my wife. I moved slightly to put myself into his line of sight, stared straight into his eyes, and at the same time sent him a mental image of him and his wife standing in front of a judge in a divorce hearing. He almost fell over. Two men walking by him at that moment steadied him for a second, glanced in our direction, and then walked out.

Still chuckling, I returned to Laura's side feeling a little more secure. I really was getting jumpy, if I was beginning to pick up the thoughts of every man who found my wife's behind attractive. That could easily be an awful lot of men. She has a great ass! Laura looked at me as I walked up next to her and said, "What's so funny?"

"Tell you later, but we may have to buy you some baggy pants."

She looked at me as if I had lost my mind and said, "What?"

I was laughing so hard by now that I was beginning to draw puzzled stares, from the people in line behind us. I managed to choke out, "Never mind!" and picked up our boarding passes. I took Laura's arm and headed us towards the departure gate, still laughing. She was laughing too by now and hitting me on the arm and saying, "You are a crazy person! Do you know that? I don't know what I see in you sometimes."

This made me laugh even harder and I said, "Maybe not, but I know what men see in you!"

So we boarded the plane arm in arm, not even vaguely aware that we had indeed been watched. Outside the terminal the two agents, assigned by Wilkinson to keep tabs on us, were at that moment reporting to him.

"Yes sir, they should be boarding the plane right now."

"What do you mean, they should be? Aren't you watching them?"

"Well sir, we were, but the guy suddenly got to acting kinda funny. He kept looking around the airport, like he was looking for someone. We were watching them from the telephone booths, but he started staring at people on the phones, one by one. We remembered what you told us about making sure we were not discovered, so rather than take a chance, we left. We almost ran into some drunk on the way out. When we turned to glance back at the subject, he was staring straight at us. So we got out as fast as we could and called you right away. They were getting their boarding passes when we left, so they should be on the plane by now."

"Good work. You did right not to take any chances. Stay there the rest of today and get a flight out tomorrow."

So, they were on their way home, which meant that by this time tomorrow, he should be happily gathering evidence on their every move. Good! He was never one who liked to wait. He could be patient beyond belief, when it was called for, but he never liked it. So, the guy was acting like he was looking for someone, eh? That might not be good news. If those two assholes had somehow let this man discover that he was being watched, Wilkinson would skin them alive. If anything should happen now to make them suspicious, they could disappear forever, and that just would not do! He might never get another opportunity like this again in his lifetime. So, he called up the men stationed at the surveillance sight and told them that he was on his way. He put them on alert and made certain that no one would be anywhere near the subject's property.

The flight home was uneventful and we dozed most of the time. By the time we actually got back to our house, we were both tired of traveling for a while. We unpacked and I started fixing supper, while Laura was taking a shower. After eating, we watched a little of the videos we had taken during our trip. As I sat there watching them, something was tickling the back of my brain. There was something I was not quite catching that my subconscious mind was picking up, and it was giving me holy hell for being so dense.

Laura had finally had enough for the day and asked me to turn off the VCR and TV, so we could go to bed. I reached for the remote control to turn off the video and hit the pause button, instead of the stop button, by mistake. Did I say by mistake? Some mistake! There on the TV screen in front of me was a still picture of two men. This was a section of video that we had taken during one of our shopping expeditions. I knew they looked familiar, but it took me a few seconds to figure out where I had seen them before. In the airport, they were the two men, who had bumped into the guy ogling Laura's ass. Ok, a strange coincidence, but not too much so. So, why were all the alarm bells going off in my head again?

I told Laura to go ahead up to bed and I would be there soon. I rewound the video and started doing a fast forward search. There they were again, both men, next to a waterfall. Again, on the beach, and once again at an outdoor cafe we ate in. I turned off the VCR and television. I had seen enough to know that we had been followed during the whole trip. This would explain my uneasy feelings during the vacation. The question was who were they, and why were they following us? I had a feeling that I knew the answer to both questions, but had no clue how to prove it, or what to do about it.

As I headed up the stairs to the bedroom, I resolved to make a trip to Godhood School tomorrow and have a little chat with The Boss. I needed some answers, or at least some guidance in this, and I could think of no better place to start. I also decided not to say anything to Laura about what I had discovered, until I had a better idea of what to do about it. One thing was certain though. I would not go to sleep this night, until I had done some things to make sure we were safe for the night.

Laura fell asleep quickly, once I got into bed. When I was sure that she would not be waking up easily, I slipped out of body and took some precautions. First, I checked thoroughly for any human life signs in the house, and found no one but Laura and I. Then, I changed all the glass in the windows into a bulletproof plastic. Next, I caused the wood of the doors to meld with the wood of the door frames at a molecular level. They looked exactly the same, but nothing short of an explosion could get them open now.

Last of all, I covered the entire exterior of the house with an invisible network of crisscrossing lines of energy. Any physical contact with the exterior of the house, by anything larger than a small bird, would instantly turn on every light in the house and set off our burglar alarm. Satisfied that we were secure for the night, I returned to my body and finally went to sleep.

What I did not know was that Richard Wilkinson had been watching us ever since we had gotten home. He had followed our every move through the numerous video cameras hidden throughout the house. He had watched carefully as I had gone back through the video and stopped time after time on shots of the two agents who had been following us. He had become so angry that he threw his ever present cup of coffee against the wall and shattered it.

"Fuck!!! God damn it!!"

He jumped up and stalked out of the cabin and paced back and forth in the cool night air, in a total rage. Damn the man! How lucky could one person be, or was it luck? The more he thought about it, the more convinced he became that luck had nothing to do with it. He opened the door to the cabin and saw one of the agents cleaning up the mess from the shattered cup. Ignoring them all, he walked over to the table, picked up another cup, filled it with coffee, and walked back out again.

He stood in the dark and stared up at the sky, as he sipped from the cup. There was no moon out tonight and the stars were brilliant in the heavens. There were no city lights near enough to where they were to wash out the view. Gradually he calmed down enough to think rationally again. He had been ready to activate the gas canisters hidden in the house and just take his chances on catching them unprepared. As he thought about it, he decided to wait just a little longer. If the guy had been alerted to his plans, then it would serve no purpose to play all his cards now. If the guy was merely suspicious, then he did not want to make any mistakes that could confirm the man's suspicions. No, playing the waiting game was still his best course at this point in time.

He continued to watch the sky for a while longer. Who were these freaks he was chasing? What must it be like to be one of them? His thoughts took him on a short excursion into the fantasy world of total power. To be able to force your will on others, to be able to fly, to be invisible, what a concept! He thought about all the changes that he would make in the world, if he had such powers available to him. Could it be possible to coerce one of these people to do his bidding? How could he manage to control one of them? What could he have or take from them that they would want badly enough to guarantee him not only their cooperation, but his safety as well? He took another sip of coffee only to find that it had grown cold. Ok, so he would return to the cabin, get some fresh coffee, and watch them for a while longer. Maybe an idea would come to him.

As he watched the man get into bed for the night, he could not help but notice the tenderness he showed toward his wife. In some ways he envied him this woman. She was not bad to look at and she seemed to really care for him. His own relationships with women had been necessarily limited to one night stands. In his business you could not afford to get too close to anyone. It created a weak point where your enemies could get to you.

A weak point! Yes, yes, a weak point. He was so elated he laughed out loud. It startled the agents in the room with him. He normally only laughed when someone was in trouble.

"Watch them carefully. Call me immediately, if anything unusual happens or if they should get out of bed."

He heard a chorus of "Yes sirs" as he walked out of the room. He was happy for the first time in a while. He knew now how to gain the upper hand on this guy. All he needed was the right opportunity to make it happen, and that would come. Just play the waiting game, and watch. He walked into the back room and lay down on the cot. He had not slept for a couple of days now, and even the coffee, he had just consumed, could not keep him awake any longer. He was asleep with a smile on his face in minutes.

11.

There are no accidents. Even the most insignificant gesture of the hand can change the course of your life.
The Book of Life

The night passed without incident. Nothing disturbed our rest and no alarms were raised. I rose early and started preparing breakfast for us. Laura woke to the smells of bacon and coffee, and joined me in the kitchen, just as I was finishing up. Just before leaving bed, I had popped out of body long enough to undo the precautions of the night before. I did not want Laura to open the front door and have all hell break loose. I still was not ready to talk to her about this yet. I did not really have anything to offer except hunches. After I talked to The Boss, I would sit down with her and fill her in on what I had learned.

Meanwhile, it was the beginning of a beautiful day. I had opened the windows in the kitchen and dining room, and there was a slight breeze. The sky was a brilliant blue with only some small, fluffy clouds scattered across the horizon. There were birds singing in a tree not too far from the window, and if I listened hard enough, I could hear the stream that ran behind the house. I felt a gentle touch on my shoulder and turned to find a pair of open arms waiting for me. She kissed me and said, "Good morning sweetheart! You're up early. Did you sleep ok?"

"Yes, I slept fine. There's just a lot I want to get done today. Besides, it's always worth getting up early just to watch you sleep. It never ceases to amaze me how peaceful and serene you look."

I brushed a stray strand of hair out of her eyes, and kissed the tip of her nose. As I pulled her closer, she wriggled against me for a moment, then formed an "O" with her lips, giggled, and said, "Oh yeah, you're awake all right! Is there something alive in your pants, or are you just glad to see me?"

"Both!"

She placed her right thigh in between my legs and moved it up and down a couple of times and said, "Are you sure you don't want to go back to bed for a while? Breakfast can wait, can't it?"

I looked into her eyes and melted. We never made it to the bedroom. In fact, we never left the kitchen. I do not normally like to rush love making, but every once in a while, a quickie can be very exciting. This was one of those times! Laura is the only woman I have ever been with that really enjoys sex in the morning. I always have, but none of the other women I had been involved with ever did. It could be very frustrating at times. That morning we were like animals in heat. It was a good thing that we had bought a really sturdy kitchen table.

It ended with us both naked and her sitting on my lap facing me, with one leg on either side of the chair, and both arms wrapped around my neck. I sometimes think I may be more animal than human because of my sense of smell. I have a very sensitive nose and can actually identify some people strictly by their smell. Also, certain people give off different smells depending on their mood. The odor given off by Laura during and after sex is the most intoxicating perfume I have ever encountered. I kissed her neck and face, inhaling huge lungs full of the smell of her. She clung to me as if I were a life preserver and she was adrift on the ocean.

"Oh God, that was good! Damn, honey! If you don't stop that, I'm gonna make you do it all over again, I swear! I have never in my life ever experienced anything like you. How do you know exactly where and how to touch me, to make me lose my mind like that? Men are not supposed to be that in tune with a woman's needs."

I took my tongue out of her ear and said, "Look who's

talking! Did your mama forget to tell you that women are not supposed to enjoy sex that much? You're only supposed to use it to control us animalistic males."

"Oh, yeah? I'll show you control bud."

I will not even try to describe what she did to me then, in that position, with what part of her anatomy. It was, however, perfectly executed, and eminently successful. I reached for her and she jumped up and started running, that perfect ass bouncing up and down as she ran, putting the finishing touches to her little maneuver. Like Pavlov's dog, I salivated and ran after her. Up the stairs we ran and into the bedroom, laughing like five year old kids.

About a mile away, our every move had been followed by several pairs of eyes. Wilkinson and the other two agents, on watch, had their eyes glued to the screens. He could tell from watching the agents' body language that they were turned on. He could hardly blame them. Those two had been putting on quite a show. Now, here they were, at it again; this time in the shower. He was beginning to become aroused himself, so he pulled his eyes from the screen and got another cup of coffee. He could hear one of the agents say to the other, "Man, I would give my left nut to spend some time with her like that!"

Wilkinson turned slowly and faced them, sipped at his

coffee, and quietly said, "And if you ever try it, that is exactly what it will cost you."

That was the end of any such comments. Wilkinson returned to drinking his coffee, and the others went back to watching the screens in silence, and sweating. He hoped that they would not have to spend an entire day watching such performances. If so, he might just have to go out and find a hooker tonight. As for the rest of them, well, let them do whatever it took to get it out of their systems, as long as it did not endanger the mission.

Meanwhile, we had finally exited from the shower and were drying off in the bedroom. I could easily have spent the rest of the day there with her, but I had things that must get done. Laura's safety might depend on it, and that was something that I dared not put off. So, we finished dressing, and went back down to try to salvage something of the now very cold breakfast I had prepared earlier.

One of the agents reached into his shirt pocket and produced a pack of cigarettes. He lit one and handed the pack to his partner. As he also started to light one, Wilkinson reached over and blew out the match.

"If you're going to both smoke at the same time, you are not going to do it in here. Do it outside, and come straight back as soon as you are finished."

"Are you sure, sir? We can wait if you like."

Wilkinson sighed and said, "No, everything seems pretty quiet right now. I think I can handle it for a few minutes, but don't take too long. I may want to go into town to have breakfast today."

They both bobbed their heads and muttered a quick, "Thank you, sir!" as they left. Wilkinson settled down in front of the monitor and sipped at his coffee. Thank God, they seemed to be heading back down to the kitchen again. Of course, that was no guarantee that it would not start all over again. After all, that was where the whole thing had originally started. He reached down and turned up the volume, so that he was sure that he could hear what they were saying.

"So, what have you got in store for today, now that you have gotten your husbandly duties taken care of, for the moment?"

"I have decided to take your advice, and go see the Boss."

Wilkinson's ears pricked up at that. Boss? This guy did not work. Who would an unemployed, filthy rich man consider his boss to be?

"How long will you be gone? I'm afraid I will be a little nervous until you return."

I smiled and took her hand gently between mine, and kissed it.

"I'm never sure where the Boss is concerned. You know how it is with Him. One thing just kind of leads to another, and the next thing you know ....."

"Yes, I know. A week has gone by."

She was smiling, but I could tell that she was about half serious.

"I will do my very best not to be gone a few weeks. You know, you could come with me. That would solve the problem very nicely."

She frowned at me and stamped her foot like a little girl, who is not getting her way.

"Oh, sure! Come hang out with you and God, while you talk shop. That sounds like a real fun time!"

Of course, she could not keep up the act for any length of

time. She finally broke down and started laughing at me. She walked over and sat down on my lap again and said, "I'm sorry hon. I don't mean to make things difficult for you. I will be all right! You know that. I have taken care of myself for most of my life, and I can do it now for however long it takes. You know I support you in this! Go! Do what you have to do. Godhood school starts for you today. I may even give you an apple to take to the teacher, if you are good."

Fuck!!! God damn it to hell! The fucking tape was not on.

"Cock suckers! Get your worthless asses in here!"

They came in on a dead run, guns drawn, eyes darting back and forth, trying to see what had set him off. When they saw no immediate danger in the room, they turned to Wilkinson and said, "What is it, sir? What happened?"

He was on his feet in a blur and his stiletto was in his hand. He laid the tip against Simms' Adams apple, and veritably spit the words out.

"Which one of you soon to be dickless wonders, forgot to turn on the tape?"

"Sir, the tape on machine one must have reached the end, while we were outside. It had been recording all night. You see the red light flashing on the control panel? That means that machine one has finished and machine two needs to be started. If you had hit the record button on machine two, everything would have continued with no interruption."

The knife bit slightly into the skin and Wilkinson's lips pulled back into a snarl, as he said, "So, you're saying it was my fault? Is that what you are saying, agent?"

"No, no sir! It was entirely my fault, sir. I take full responsibility. I should not have left my post for even a minute, without making sure that everything was covered."

It was clear from the way the man was sweating and holding his breath that he fully expected to die here. Yet, he had accepted responsibility for his actions anyway. Wilkinson liked that. It showed both a lot of guts, and a willingness to take the blame for him, when it counted most. That could be very useful.

He let the man go and returned his stiletto to the sleeve sheath. It really had been his own fault. He had become so caught up in what was being said that he had allowed his concentration to wander. That was a dangerous thing for a man in his line of work to do. Simms walked over to machine two and started the tape. He looked at Wilkinson and said, "Did we miss something important, sir?"

Wilkinson straightened his tie and tucked his shirt back into his pants, as he returned to the monitor. He picked up his coffee cup, took a slow sip, and then turned to face the others.

"We go on full alert as of this moment. Get everyone back here on the double. I do not want one second of time to go unrecorded from this point forward. No one, I repeat, no one will smoke, eat drink, piss, or even fart unless someone else is glued to the controls. Is that crystal clear, gentlemen?"

"Yes, sir!"

"Then get to it! Our friend is planning a trip to talk to God, at a place called Godhood School. The woman will be staying at home. As soon as he is gone, I want that place gassed and her taken. I want him followed to where ever he goes, and death will find whoever loses him in the process. Now move!!!"

Unaware of all the commotion going on just a mile away, we sat down at the table to finish breakfast. Again, until I was surer of what was going on, I was not going to upset Laura any more than she already was. I had no intention of being gone even overnight, much less for weeks. If need be, Godhood School would just have to wait, until I got things a little more under control. I was not sure exactly what it would consist of, but I was sure that it would be very serious work. I could not afford to have my attention on the house and Laura, while something vital slipped right by me.

However, I did want to talk to the Boss and get his take on all of this. Besides, I had grown very fond of Him during my time trip back to Jesus' time. I was curious to see what appearance he was using in my time. Also, I wondered how he would react to me. For me, it had been just a few days since we had spent several weeks together. For him, almost two thousand years had passed, or had it?

This time travel stuff could have you thinking inside out, if you weren't careful. If I could time trip, so could he. Yet, he had to be there during all the intervening centuries to continue to guide man's destiny, didn't he? Hmm! Question number one for whoever would be teaching Godhood School.

"..... and then I married a Martian, and had chickens for my earache. Excuse me sir! Am I boring you?"

I blinked and gave her a blank stare for a second, and then uttered the ever intelligent line, "Huh?"

"Oh, that's it mister. Get out now! Go do your thing and get it over with, so I can have my husband back, for a while at least."

"Okay, okay. I'm going."

"All right, places everyone! He is on the move. Get Pursuit One on line and have them pick him up, as soon as he leaves the road to their property. Simms, follow him out of the house with the cameras and make sure you let Pursuit One know, which vehicle he will be using."

I walked slowly upstairs towards the bedroom, with a drag to my steps. I had to do this, but I felt that something was wrong again.

"Where the fuck is he going? The bitch kissed him goodbye and told him to get going. He said, "Goodbye, I'll see you later." and then he walks upstairs?"

I reached the bedroom and lay down on the bed. The hair on the back of Wilkinson's neck began to stand up. His heart was pounding. Laura walked into the room, just as I was closing my eyes and said, "Have a good trip, hon. I'll see you when you get back."

As I left my body, she bent down and kissed my cheek. I could not resist. I materialized my right hand, as she turned around and headed for the door, and pinched her ass. She whipped around and started laughing out loud, when she saw the disembodied hand waving goodbye.

"Got you! Got you!! I got your ass, mister!!! Gas the bitch.

Now! I want her bound, gagged, drugged and on her way to a safe house, within fifteen minutes at the outside. He could return at any time."

The agents were looking at Wilkinson, as if he had lost his mind.

"Return from where, sir? He hasn't left yet. See? He's still right there in bed."

I left the house through the east wall and headed straight up. I took one last look at the house and grabbed hold of space/time and twisted. I slipped effortlessly into the dimension where Godhood School was located. Funny, I never noticed that popping sound before, when I did this. It sounded kind of like a firecracker off in the distance.

Wilkinson had shot Simms. The man was bleeding a lot from the left arm, but the wound was far from fatal. Wilkinson now had the gun aimed at the agent standing closest to him.

"The next cock sucker that questions one of my orders, dies!"

"Releasing gas, sir."

I arrived at Godhood School and walked into the reception

area. Yes, God has a reception area, and a secretary. How else can He screen His visitors and see only those He wants to see, when He wants to see them? You didn't think He makes His own appointments and answers His own phone, did you? Okay, so I'm kidding about the phone.

Laura felt suddenly very dizzy for a quick instant, and then passed out. Her last conscious thought was, "Oh no! My poor husband!"

"Now! Get in there and get her out. Move!"

I had this very bizarre feeling that Laura was in danger, I was just heading for the door to leave, when the secretary said, "Sir? He will see you now."

I hesitated and the man looked at me rather strangely and said, "The Boss says He is ready now, sir. Please do not keep Him waiting."

The feeling of wrongness was increasing by the minute, and I knew it had something to do with Laura. If I left now, I might or might not be able to figure out what the problem was. If on the other hand I went in and talked to the Boss, maybe He could help me find a permanent solution to the problem, whatever it was. I swallowed my fear for the moment and walked into the office.

12.

If you find only
evil in the world,
it is because that
is what you expect
to find. Look again
with love in your
heart and tell me
what you see.
The Book of Life

The office was huge! No, that's an understatement. The office was monumental! It was more like a building within a building. There was red carpet under my feet that was about three feet wide. This ran straight down the center of the room toward the far end. On either side of the carpet were marble pillars, about every 20 feet. The floor itself was made of mahogany and was polished to a soft, gentle sheen.

There were paintings hanging on the walls of many different historical figures, some of which I recognized, and many of which I did not. There were also some landscapes that were either painted by someone with a vivid imagination, on drugs, or else they were of another planet. At the far end of the red carpeting was a large desk, made of some material I could not identify from this far away.

Behind it was a large chair that was turned away from me, so that all I could see was the back of the chair. I could not tell if there was anyone in it or not, from this angle.

As impressive as all of this was, it did not startle me nearly as much as what I saw through the ....., I guess you would call them windows! They were about 30 feet high and about 5 feet wide. There was no glass or glass like material in them at all. They appeared to be open to the outside, and what an outside!

The sky was a blood red, with pastel blue and pink clouds formed into intertwined ribbons. A red giant sun was just beginning to come up over the horizon, or was just going down; it was hard to tell which. There was a gentle breeze blowing through the office, which contained scents that I had never encountered before. The air was around 85° and so dry that I would have been surprised if there was any humidity at all. In the distance I could see the outlines of what appeared to be a jagged and unbelievably high mountain range. The countryside, between us and the mountains, was hilly and very barren.

This could not be real! I had just come in from outside, and there was nothing out there that even vaguely approached this. Also, this entire building seen from outside was not much larger than this office appeared to be. There was something going on here that defied all the normal laws of space, as I knew them. If I concentrated and shifted my sight slightly in the manner that I do to time travel, I could see that something had indeed been done to the space/time continuum in the vicinity of the office door. It looked as though the door was actually a portal to another place and time.

"It is an amazing view, is it not?"

I turned to see the man, whom I had come to know as Jesus of Nazareth, standing next to me. I had been so absorbed in looking around that I had not noticed him walking up to me. He looked exactly the same as the last time I had seen him. I smiled and held out my hand. He laughed and hugged me instead. I was surprised by this open display of affection, but it pleased me no end. As I had said before, I had come to care a great deal for this man in the time we had spent together. It was good to know that he felt the same way.

"Yes, it is indeed an amazing view. Just exactly where and when are we, anyway?"

He laughed that deep and melodious laugh of his and said, "This is my home planet, as it was about ten thousand years prior to the year of my birth. Just how long ago that was, I am not willing to admit."

He took my arm and steered me toward a corner of the office, where there were chairs and a small table next to one of the windows. I could see what appeared to be coffee in one cup and some unidentifiable liquid in another, there on the table. I assumed that the coffee was for me.

"So, my friend, how are you? It has been a long time for me, since we last talked. I have sorely missed your company and your humorous outlook on life."

I blushed slightly at this. It is not every day that you talk to God in person. Now add to that him saying he has missed you. I think you would blush with pleasure also. We sat down in the chairs and he motioned for me to pick up the cup of coffee.

"I have missed you as well. I am fine, although I do have some concerns that I wanted to discuss with you."

He laughed briefly at this.

"Ah, my friend, you have not changed. You cut straight to the chase when something bothers you, don't you? Yes. I am aware of your concerns. Your love for Laura and your fear for her well being are admirable. However, there are many events coming together at the same time now. There is some cause for concern on your part, but not necessarily in the way you think."

"Then you are aware that Laura and I are being watched?"

"Yes, you are."

"And you know who it is that is watching us?"

"Oh yes. I am intimately familiar with the situation."

I was getting that feeling again. The hair on the back of my neck was standing up and every nerve in my body was screaming, danger!

"I get the distinct impression that you are not telling me everything. I am also very sure that Laura is in some kind of danger, even as we speak. Are you going to help me? Can you help me?"

"The answer to both questions is, yes. However, you are correct that I cannot tell you everything at this point. As I said, there are a lot of things happening right now. There are many life paths converging and becoming intertwined, with several possible futures emerging from that convergence. At the center of this whirlwind of events stands one man, you! What you do and how you react to what is about to happen will have repercussions down through the ages."

"Yes, I will help you. I will do all that I can to prepare you for what is to come, but I will not reveal the future to you. Do you trust me?"

There was no hesitation. There may be many things in life that I am not sure of, but this was not one of them.

"Yes! You know I do!"

He smiled.

"Then come with me my friend. I have some things I must show you."

"What about Laura? She is in danger! I must help her!"

He looked at me in a way that spoke volumes about pain and the understanding of it. There was a tear rolling down his cheek, as he laid his hand on my shoulder.

"Laura is where she must be. She also is caught up in this vortex of events. All things in their own time, my friend. Come!"

That tear in his eye frightened me more than anything I had seen yet. He knew that I loved him. He knew how much I loved Laura. I also believed that he loved me, and had only my best interests at heart. I had come seeking his guidance. He was my God. What else could I do?

"Where do we go?"

He suddenly got a faraway look in his eyes and said in a very quiet voice, "So, it has begun. A moment, my friend."

He stood absolutely still for about two minutes. He never moved at all. I would swear that he neither blinked nor breathed during that time. I was beginning to wonder what was going on, when he suddenly smiled at me and said, "All right, let us begin. It is time you had some history lessons."

He touched my shoulder with one hand and the office dissolved around us. We were standing at the top of a hill overlooking a valley populated by two groups of people separated by a small, sparse stand of trees. It appeared to be two opposing armies arranging their ranks for a conflict. Judging by the armor, the horsemen, and ranks of archers, I would guess we were somewhere in Europe during the Renaissance. I must admit that this period in history had always fascinated me. The idea of knighthood, chivalry, and the moral code of conduct for these knights had seemed to be very appealing. If there must be war, at least in that time, it was limited pretty much to hand to hand combat. It had seemed much preferable to the means of mass destruction we had since developed.

"Why are we here?"

"You are here to observe, and to learn."

"Learn what?"

He laughed at me and said, "Among other things, patience, I hope."

Okay, I can take a hint. I shut up and we watched. We did not have long to wait. As the trumpets blared and the first waves of men charged toward each other, we floated closer to them. It took me a few seconds to realize why no one had noticed us. I keep forgetting that we are not visible to anyone, unless we will it so. When we finally stopped, we were in the center of the action. I will never forget it.

The men were screaming at the top of their lungs, as they ran toward each other. When they met, the sound of metal on metal was added as sword met sword. Then the cries of pain were added all around us. The sounds of the death rattle were next. I guess it had never occurred to me that death by sword was not an easy thing.

A sword is a cutting weapon mostly. Death can come from being stabbed by one, but that is usually only after one has been disabled by hacking into ones' flesh repeatedly. Hands were cut off. Legs gashed to the point of no longer being able to support the body's weight. Stomachs are sliced open and the bowels spilled onto the ground. The spurting of severed arteries was everywhere.

The ground around them became so soaked with blood that it began to form red mud. Then the thunder of horses' hooves was added to the tumult around us. We could see great plumes of steam in the cold morning air coming from the horses' nostrils, as they ran. The ground began to tremble under the feet of the infantry men, as the horses and riders approached. Covered in blood, they stood their ground and waited. All around them lay the bodies of the dead and the dying. Men crying for their mothers, as their life spurted from their bodies in little fountains of death. Others were wounded so badly that they could only lay on their backs staring up at the gray sky over head, and wait for the agony to end.

Then the horses collided with the men. Some of the foot soldiers were thrown aside by the weight of the horses, as if they were rag dolls. Others were sliced almost in half by the combined force of the blow from the sword of a mounted soldier and the added weight and speed of the horse. Some of the horses were hit by the swords of the infantry, and then the sounds of their screams were added to the cacophony of death around us.

The worst part of all was the look in the eyes of the men as they fought and died. At first it was fear. Then slowly, as more and more of their friends and comrades were killed, the fear in their eyes was replaced with blood lust. It grew constantly until the very air was charged with it. Their pupils dilated and their breath came faster and faster. They began to take real pleasure in inflicting pain and mortal wounds. I could hear their thoughts as they lost their humanity to the hate that consumed them.

"Bastards! You killed James! I will kill you all!!! Only a demon from hell would serve that king! Death to you all! I will burn your villages, rape your women, and kill your babies! We will wipe the stain of you from the earth entire!!!"

On and on it went. Not just for a few minutes, but hour after hour of hack and stab, then on to the next. They became so tired that they were having trouble holding on to their weapons now. They were covered from head to toe with blood, some of it their own, most of it not. The white hot heat of their lust had died down now to a numbness. Most of those, who were still alive, had not really expected to be so by this time. Most were professional soldiers and knew the life expectancy of their profession. Now, they just wanted to make it to the end of the battle. The fear was back again.

I had been too close to it for too long and could not stand the smell of blood any longer. I had backed off to the top of one of the hills, where one of the armies had their command post set up. The Boss had followed me, but had not spoken a word since the battle had begun. It was pretty much over now. The recall signal had been given by the invading army, and the defenders had chased them part way up the hill. When the victorious general had finally been satisfied that the enemy had been completely routed, he ordered his men to abandon the chase.

The survivors came straggling back to their own lines. A ragged, emotionless, half hearted cheer was raised when their commander saluted them from the top of the hill. I wandered among them as they returned. The emotions they were feeling now were much different than they were at the beginning of the battle. They looked down over the valley they had just left and wept. The ground was covered with the dead. The small stream that ran through the middle of the battle field was running red with the blood of friend and foe alike. The crows and ravens had already descended on the bodies and had begun to feed. The ground had become so soaked in blood that the worms had come up out of the earth like they often did after a heavy rain. The sun was beginning to go down in the west and even the sky now appeared to be stained red. I could imagine no scene from hell that could be more frightening.

Now the priests and the medics began their gruesome duties of sifting through the carnage for survivors, who might be healed, and to give Last Rights to those who could not. There was a new sound now floating across the evening air. It was the sound of countless men crying and praying. The few left on the battle field still alive would not be so for long. The medics were not true trained healers and could really do no more than sew up wounds and set bones. When they did not know what else to do, they would apply leaches, which often made the death of the wounded man a certainty.

As I watched them go about their chores, I noticed members of the defeated army starting to arrive to search for their own wounded and to reclaim the bodies of their fallen comrades. The burial details of both armies worked side by side to clean up the remains of the day's insanity. I saw a boy from the victorious army bent over, vomiting as he was overcome by the scene around him. Standing next to him was an older man from the defeated army, with his arm around the young man's shoulder, trying to console him.

"It's okay, lad. There is no shame! What sane man would not be sickened by what we do?"

"Does it ever get any easier?"

The older man looked away and his shoulders hunched, as he replied.

"Only for those who have lost their souls. What are you doing here, son?"

The boy stood up and wiped his mouth with the back of his hand. There was just enough light left to see the gleam of tears in his eyes.

"Like all the boys of our village, I was tired of being a farmer. I longed to see new lands and to cover myself with riches and glory in battle. When this campaign started, I was still too young and inexperienced to be a soldier, so I volunteered to go along and do whatever needed doing. My mother cried, when I left, and begged me to stay. She had already lost a husband and one son to the wars and did not want to be alone in her old age. I laughed at her foolishness then. I would give much to see her smiling at me now."

The boy began to cry and the older man reached out and took him into his arms. He held him there and stroked his hair while he cried' as he would have done for his own child.

"Go home, son. Go be with your mother. Go and court the young maidens. Marry and raise boys of your own. Go, and live the life you were meant to live. Remember this day and practice war no more."

The boy backed away from the older man and wiped at his eyes. He held out his hand to the enemy, shook it, and then went back to burying the dead. I reached into his mind and heard him planning his trip home for that very night. I touched the mind of the enemy soldier, who had befriended him, and found grief, and regret for his fallen friends, and his own dead sons. He wept for the lost innocence of the boy whom he had just met, and for the time alone he had subjected his wife to.

I felt a hand on my shoulder and turned to see the Boss staring into my eyes with a look of concern.

"How do you stand it?" I said. "How can you have lived through tens of thousands of years of this kind of brutality and still care about us? Why have you not abandoned us to our own insanity? What do you find in us to care about?"

He shook his head and looked more serious than I had ever seen him before.

"You have not learned the full lesson yet."

He touched my shoulder and we floated up to about a thousand feet above the valley and stopped. He turned to me and said, "You must learn the worth of your people. Short of living among them, as long as I have, the only way to do so is to become them for a while. Not just one person, but a large number. You must experience the potential of the race for greatness as well as for destruction. I will help guide you through it, but you must surrender to it completely."

I stood there and opened myself up to everything going on around me. For the first time, since I had discovered my new abilities, I gave up control and just let the lives and emotions of those around me enter my consciousness all at once. I made no attempt at control of any kind. I just let it happen. The flood of it! For a time, I was completely lost. There was no me, only us! All the lives, all the pain, all the joy, the deaths, the births, the total sum of the life experiences of everyone there all came together in me. We traded our individual identities for a collective.

After I had absorbed all that their lives had to offer, I could feel Him guiding me forward into the future, but not a normal time trip. The generations of descendents from those I was joined with now came into the equation as well. Musicians, poets, priests, kings, doctors, rulers, thieves, murderers, saints and sinners, all were there and included. We traveled into the dim future of humanity through the lives of it's members, all at the same time. Now there were no details at all. There were too many people, too many lives to separate them out into anything more than what had become a symphony of discovery. Upward it soared to the final crescendo that is the ultimate destiny of man. I was there, and I know where we are headed, but there are no words for it.

In the end, I would have been lost forever in the wonder of it, if the Boss had not forcibly called me back to myself. We were back in his office sitting in the chairs and he was watching me intently. I threw my arms about him and wept for joy. I could not speak, but the tears flowed like the river of time. I was slipping away again, when he spoke.

"So, my son! Do you now know what I see in you?"

All I could manage was, "Oh dear God!"

13.

<u>Love is not</u>

<u>explained. Love</u>

<u>simply is</u>.

<u>The Book of Life</u>

We sat and talked for a while longer about inconsequential things. Slowly, I gained enough control over my emotions to be able to return to thoughts of the present. Finally, I said that I was sure he had other things to do, and I needed to get home to check on Laura. I said that I would return soon to start Godhood School, and then He startled me by saying that I had already started. He shook my hand as I left and I could have sworn that there was a tear in his eye.

As I came within sight of our house, I knew that Laura was not there. I have been very sensitive to her presence for some time now, and what I had been through today had heightened that perception. I checked the garage and both vehicles were there, so she had not driven away. I entered the house through the roof and came down in our bedroom. There was my body, right where I had left it. I stretched my senses throughout the house and detected a male presence in the living room. Other than my own body on the bed, his was the only living presence in the house. I moved toward him.

He was sitting on the edge of the couch with his legs crossed casually and sipping a cup of coffee. He seemed awfully at ease for someone who was, at the very least, guilty of burglary. I could easily have entered his mind and discovered everything I wanted to know, but I found the thought somehow distasteful. So I decided to take a somewhat different approach. I returned to the bedroom and checked my body carefully to make certain there were no booby traps of any kind attached to it. When I was sure it was safe, I reentered my body, took an unloaded revolver from the night stand, and headed for the living room. The gun was for effect only. I was not in the least afraid of the man downstairs, physically.

He must have heard me coming, for as I reached the bottom of the stairs, he stood up and faced me. He was a tall man, about six feet or six foot one, slender but muscular, salt and pepper hair, and steel gray eyes. He was a very attractive man, who looked to be somewhere in his early fifties, but he gave off a sense that he was still very agile, and very dangerous. He moved slowly, almost arrogantly, but there was an underlying tension to him that said that this could change instantaneously to lightning quick motion. He reminded me of a cat ignoring a mouse, pretending to be asleep, until it was foolish enough to get within range. I had no doubt at all that this was the person responsible for the problems Laura and I had recently been having. It was time to get some answers.

I pointed the gun at him and said, "Where is my wife?"

He actually smiled at me.

"I would have made book that those would have been your first words. Most people would have asked who I was, how I got in, what did I want, but I know you pretty well by now. Your concern is first and foremost for your wife, isn't it?"

"Okay, if it will make you feel better. Who are you, how did you get in here, and what do you want?"

He laughed, and sat back down on the couch.

"I do so enjoy a man who can have a sense of humor in the face of danger. Please, do sit down. We have much to discuss, and please put away that gun. I know you will not use it. You have no need of weapons to defend yourself, and I know it."

I laid the revolver on a table and sat down in a chair facing him.

"I will not ask you again. Where is my wife?"

"I don't know her actual physical location at this moment. I'm sure you can verify that if you want. I would, however, advice against it. She is safe, for the moment. No one will harm her in any way what so ever, unless you force the issue. But if anything unusual happens, if I suddenly start acting as if I am in pain or distress of any kind, if you should suddenly get very still and stop moving, she is dead. So, how was your trip? Did you have a nice time at Godhood School?"

This startled me, and it must have shown on my face, for he laughed again.

"Oh yes, we have been watching you for some time now. In fact, we are being watched at this very moment. That is my insurance policy. There are video cameras in every room and the signals from them are being bounced around all over the planet. Somewhere out there, your wife is drugged and unconscious. Around her neck is a very special piece of jewelry I had made, just for her. It is constructed of only the finest new plastic explosive, and is attached to a radio controlled detonator."

"When she left here, she was handed off to several different people, transferred from one vehicle to another several times, and is now in a place I do not know the location of. That way, you have no chance of rescuing her. So you see, even if you were foolish enough to leave your body and attempt to rip her location from me, it would do you no good. Try it, and her head will be blown from her body, before you could even find the first person in the chain."

"How do I know that she is alive at all? You do not strike me as a very trustworthy person. Under the circumstances, you don't really expect me to just take your word for it, do you?"

"Certainly not! I have arranged a way to give you the proof you need. Turn on the television over there."

I walked over and turned it on, and there was Laura, obviously drugged and barely conscious, but alive.

"This could be a video tape. It proves nothing."

"Talk to her. She can see and hear you. I told you we were being watched."

"Laura, can you hear me?"

"Yes, beloved."

"Are you okay? Have they hurt you in any way?"

"No, I have not been harmed. I'm stoned to the gills, but I'm okay."

"All right. What do you want?"

"Well, what I really would like is to have you both drugged and under control, but I don't believe you would go for that, would you?"

"No!"

"Didn't think so. Okay, then we will just settle for some information for now, and maybe have you do a couple of things for me later on."

I was becoming angry!

"You say that you know something about me and the powers I possess. I tell you now that you have no conception of who and what I am, but know this. If anything, anything at all happens to my wife, I will invent a new and special hell for you alone. If you give her back to me now, we will simply disappear. I will find her, of that you can be certain."

Agent Simms watched the drama being played out on the screen before him. In the next room was the man's wife, Laura. He had made damn sure that he was the one who ended up with her. He rubbed his healing arm, where Wilkinson had shot him, and winced at the pain. The bastard had fucked him once too often.

Wilkinson looked at the man before him and brought a lifetime of experience at judging people to bear on him. The man meant exactly what he had said. He began to sweat, just a little.

It finally clicked in my head, and I knew who this man was.

"It was you! You were the one, who tortured that man 30 years ago. All he wanted to do was to help end the war in Vietnam, to maybe save some lives, and his reward was to be drugged and tortured. You were the one!"

Simms found this to be very interesting. Here was some information he had not heard before. He would wait a little longer.

Wilkinson began to be afraid. He did not like what was happening here. He was supposed to be the one in charge, not this guy.

"Don't fuck with me! I will kill her!"

I sensed his fear and played on it.

"The people, who rescued that man, they did something to you, didn't they?"

"Shut up!"

"They put you to sleep and fed you his memories of the torture, didn't they?"

Wilkinson dropped the stiletto from his sleeve sheath into his hand. His voice was becoming higher pitched now and was beginning to tremble.

"I said shut up you fucker! I'm in control here, not you!"

I could feel that there were other forces coming into play here. This must be the moment that the Boss had warned me about. Even while still in my body, I could feel the tempest coming. I felt as if there was nothing to do now, but try desperately to control what was happening here. I had to be very careful not to push him too far.

Simms was fascinated! This explained so much that he knew about Wilkinson, such as his obsession with finding these so called supermen, and his fear of sleep. He could not resist a chance to take a little revenge before the final act. He picked up the microphone and spoke.

"So, Mr. Wilkinson! These guys fucked with your brain, eh? That explains the nightmares."

Wilkinson whipped around and faced toward the television, and went into a crouch. He was sweating profusely now and he was killing mad.

"Simms? What are you doing? Where are you?"

I could tell that this was something Wilkinson had not expected. It had distracted him. Perhaps I could use this to my advantage somehow.

"I'm here, with the woman. Are you having a good time there with your new friend? I don't think he likes you very much boss."

I was losing control here.

"Whoever is there with Simms, shoot him! Kill him now! That's an order!"

"Sorry boss man. No one here but us chickens. What do you suppose this guy would do to you, if I pressed this button and this pretty little lady's head went boom?"

I spoke just loud enough for Wilkinson to hear me.

"Tell me where he is and I will save her and let you go, I swear it!"

He jerked around to face me with his lips pulled back in a snarl of rage, and screamed at me.

"I told you, I don't know where she is!"

There was no hope at all as long as I remained in my body now. This had gone beyond Wilkinson's control and the man there with Laura seemed to be intent on forcing my hand. The storm had arrived.

"Well, I would love to prolong this game for a while and watch you fall apart, but I have a feeling that this guy is going to get very pissed any second now, and I don't want to stick around for that. So, here's the deal. First I kill the bitch."

I dropped my body like a rock and started reaching through the television signal to trace it to the source.

"Then I wait to see what this guy does to you."

Wilkinson heard my body hit the floor and screamed in terror.

Simms pushed the button. Even in the midst of search, I was still watching what was happening. I was actually in more than one place at one time, for the very first time. I saw Laura's head explode. I heard Simms laugh. My world died.

I could still hear Simms talking to Wilkinson.

"Fuck it! I ain't gonna let anyone else kill you. Remember that C4 we planted in the basement? I'm gonna blow your ass to kingdom come you bastard."

Wilkinson was screaming non-stop now. Drool was running down his chin and his eyes were so dilated that there was almost no pupil showing at all. Blow up the house? Explosives? I didn't care if I died now, but somewhere deep inside me the sights and sounds of the battle that I had watched, came back to me. Too much blood! Too much death! I could not let this go on any more. The cycle of insanity must end.

"Goodbye, you fuck!"

I reached for Wilkinson and we dematerialized as the house exploded around us. We popped back into reality on the top of a mountain in Sedona. I set him down on the ground and materialized, so he could see me. He was gone. His mind had left him altogether. I went back to what was left of the house and picked up my body. It was, of course, unharmed. I had already left it before the explosion and it had been protected. I brought it back to where I had left Wilkinson, re-entered my body, sat down next to him and began to cry. Laura!

Deep from inside me the feeling welled up, until I could no longer contain it. I opened my mouth and out of it poured all the pain and grief gathered together in one word that I hurled into the cosmos, with all the force at my command.

"Why?"

I cried until my eyes would produce no more tears. Then I turned and looked at Wilkinson. He had not moved. He had urinated on himself sometime during the hours we had been there, and never even knew it. He had retreated into a place within himself, so deep that he would never return. Somehow this moved me to tears again. He had been the one responsible for hounding us all for the last 30 years. He had been responsible for Laura's capture, and in the end, for her death. But, I had seen the final worth of our species. I had been there and seen what we would become. He was one of us. He was part of the whole. I just could not bring myself to leave him this way.

I reached out and entered his body. The brain was physically undamaged, so I moved into his mind. He had no defenses that could keep me out. I found him cowering in a corner of himself, like a child locked in a dark closet. I could see him with his arms wrapped around himself, rocking back and forth and crying. I took his memories then and held them to me for a while. Then slowly, gently, I created an image to hold him. I gave him Laura. I used her image to soothe him and coax him out of himself. In the end, she took him by the hand and led him back to consciousness.

He opened his eyes and blinked at me. Then the tears started.

"You saved me? Why?"

I sighed and turned away from him, to stare out at the sunset.

"Where is the woman? She brought me back. I have to see her! Where is she?"

"I am here."

14.

<u>There are no</u>
<u>endings; only new</u>
<u>beginnings!</u>
<u>The Book of Life</u>

I turned at the sound of her voice and my heart caught fire! Dear God! Oh merciful Jesus! She lives! I was on my feet and had swept her into my arms, before I could breathe. I began to weep all over again. She was the most beautiful sight I have ever seen. I covered her in kisses, rained them down on her face like there would be no tomorrow. Ohhh! How can I tell you how I felt? The universe cannot contain the love I poured out upon her, there on top of that mountain. I touched her everywhere. I held her, squeezed her, covered every inch of her, as if to make certain that she was really there, and not a dream. I was laughing and crying all at the same time. Her tears mixed with mine, as they ran down our cheeks.

"How? I saw you die."

"Come down from there, and I'll explain it to you."

I looked toward the sound of this new voice, and found that Laura and I were floating about 20 feet above the top of the mountain. Something had happened, when I saw her again, and I was now able to fully manifest my powers, while still in my body. There was also a warm, golden light surrounding us. I looked at Wilkinson and he was staring up at us and crying. Standing next to him was the Boss. I settled us gently back to the ground and with one hand, reached out and pulled Him to us. The three of us stood there holding each other for a few moments and then Laura said, "Okay, tell him."

"Yes, quite right."

He looked at me and smiled. Clasping me on the shoulder, He said, "She never died. What you saw was a construct that I created, similar to the one I use. When they originally gassed her, I replaced her with the construct, before they arrived to pick her up. She has been safe with me the entire time."

I thought about this for a moment.

"Don't get me wrong here. I will be eternally grateful that you have saved her life, but why did you let me believe she had died? Do you have any idea what you have put me through?"

He looked at me now with that old look I had seen so many times before; the one that spoke of such an intimate knowledge of pain and suffering.

"Yes, my friend. I know. After all, I had to pass my test too."

"Test? What test?"

"Why, your final exam from Godhood School, of course."

Once again, I reached deep within and brought forth the ever intelligent, "Huh?"

Laura laughed until I thought she would burst. The Boss was all smiles from ear to ear.

"Think about it for a moment. How do you know if someone can be trusted to be given absolute power over an entire race of newly evolving beings? How do you know that they will be willing to put the needs of their charges above all else? You have been in Godhood School ever since Laura came to you that first night. Everything that has happened has been pushing you toward this day, when your moment of truth would come."

"This man had hounded you for years. He had caused harm and suffering to your wife. He had made you worry night and day for months over her safety. He finally captured her and caused her to be put to death, before your very eyes. Most people would not blame you, if you had rendered him limb from limb. In fact, that is what almost anyone else would have done, but what did you do? You saved his life. Then, as if that were not amazing enough, you looked deep enough to recognize the spark of humanity in him, and gave him back his identity. Most incredible of all, you did this by sharing with him the love of the woman he had caused to die. I call that extraordinary."

Laura beamed at me and said, "I could have told you that. Why do you think I love him so?"

"So, what happens now?"

"I would say that you have both earned a vacation. We have arranged for new identities for you. As far as everyone is concerned, you both died. I even planted a construct corpse of you in the wreckage of your house. You will not be bothered any more. When you are ready, come see me and we will get you started on your new job."

"What will you do with Wilkinson?"

The Boss gestured toward Wilkinson and he suddenly was changed in an instant. He bore not the slightest resemblance to his old self.

"Considering that his body was found at the house as well, and seeing that he has a new appearance, I would recommend that he disappear and start a new life, perhaps something outside, close to nature. You know, like maybe a Forest Ranger."

Epilogue

Jhama closed the book and pushed the chair back from the table. He sighed and stood up. What a story. He felt a presence in the room and turned to see a man standing there, who looked at him with great affection. He almost felt as if he knew this man, but could not quite remember from where.

"Hello? Who are you?"

The man laughed gently and walked toward him.

"So, what did you think of my story, Jhama?"

"Your story? You mean, you are ..."

Jhama fell to his knees and began to pray. The man walked

over and lifted him to his feet.

"Please, don't do that! You read the book. Do you not understand it? There are not really any Gods, only caretakers. I am just like you. We are all one."

"Are you truly God? I mean, our God? I mean, the God of this world?"

"Yes, Jhama."

"And this really was your true story?"

"Yes."

"Then, Lord, why reveal it to me?"

"Have you not guessed yet? The dreams, Jhama! Your people are evolving once again. You are starting the same process my people did so long ago, the same process that brought me here to your world, over one hundred thousand of your years ago. Why do you think The Sisters have talked for generations now about the significance of dreams? It is the first signs of the change. You, Jhama, are going through that change. You are the first of your people to do so. That is why I had Laura lead you here."

Jhama was bewildered, and it showed. He was tired and now he was scared as well.

"Lord, what do you wish from me?"

"You will start a new school here to help train your people, as they too begin to go through the change. Do not despair! That will be a while yet, but it has begun. You have no idea how much this pleases us. It means that we have done our jobs well and your people are on the right track."

Jhama sat back down in his chair and rubbed at his forehead.

"It is a lot to comprehend all at once."

"Yes, it is. But we have time, Jhama. Come! Let us go take supper together. Laura is waiting for us."